CHICAGO

W9-BTD-444

R02007 53493

Brett's eyes lit with amazement as the baby kicked exactly where he pressed his hand.

The look on his face was one she knew she'd never forget. Wonder. Joy.

Brett's eyes rose to meet Melissa's, and there was something else written there. It was hot and needy and had nothing whatsoever to do with the baby. Slowly, as if forcing himself, he pulled his hand away.

The feel of his fingertips just before they broke contact sent a spiraling shaft of desire through her. The pull between them was stronger. She could feel it. She knew he could, too. And though they both fought it and never spoke of it, it grew. But she was as wrong for Brett and his lifestyle as he was for hers. Besides, Brett was never going to be more to the baby than an uncle, and Melissa knew she had to stop hoping things could be different. They couldn't.

Could they?

NORTH AUSTIN BRANCH
5724 W. NORTH AVE.
CHICAGO, IL 60639

Dear Reader,

Not only does Special Edition bring you the joys of life, love and family—but we also capitalize on our authors' many talents in storytelling. In our spotlight, Christine Rimmer's exciting new miniseries, VIKING BRIDES, is the epitome of innovative reading. The first book, *The Reluctant Princess,* details the transformation of an everyday woman to glorious royal—with a Viking lover to match! Christine tells us, "For several years, I've dreamed of creating a modern-day country where the ways of the legendary Norsemen would still hold sway. I imagined what fun it would be to match up the most macho of men, the Vikings, with contemporary American heroines. Oh, the culture clash—oh, the lovely potential for lots of romantic fireworks! This dream became VIKING BRIDES." Don't miss this fabulous series!

Our Readers' Ring selection is Judy Duarte's *Almost Perfect,* a darling tale of how good friends fall in love as they join forces to raise two orphaned kids. This one will get you talking! Next, Gina Wilkins delights us with *Faith, Hope and Family,* in which a tormented heroine returns to save her family and faces the man she's always loved. You'll love Elizabeth Harbison's *Midnight Cravings,* in which a sassy publicist and a small-town police chief fall hard for each other and give in to a sizzling attraction.

The Unexpected Wedding Guest, by Patricia McLinn, brings together an unlikely couple who share an unexpected kiss. Newcomer to Special Edition Kate Welsh is no stranger to fresh plot twists, in *Substitute Daddy,* in which a heroine carries her deceased twin's baby and has feelings for the last man on earth she should love—her snooty brother-in-law.

As you can see, we have a story for every reader's taste. Stay tuned next month for six more top picks from Special Edition!

Sincerely,

Karen Taylor Richman
Senior Editor

Please address questions and book requests to:
Silhouette Reader Service
U.S.: 3010 Walden Ave., P.O. Box 1325, Buffalo, NY 14269
Canadian: P.O. Box 609, Fort Erie, Ont. L2A 5X3

Substitute Daddy

KATE WELSH

NORTH AUSTIN BRANCH
5724 W. NORTH AVE.
CHICAGO, IL 60639

Silhouette®

SPECIAL EDITION™

Published by Silhouette Books

America's Publisher of Contemporary Romance

If you purchased this book without a cover you should be aware
that this book is stolen property. It was reported as "unsold and
destroyed" to the publisher, and neither the author nor the
publisher has received any payment for this "stripped book."

To my daughter, Heather.

May you and your hero live happily ever after.
Happy first anniversary.

Mom

 SILHOUETTE BOOKS

ISBN 0-373-24542-4

SUBSTITUTE DADDY

Copyright © 2003 by Kate Welsh

All rights reserved. Except for use in any review, the reproduction
or utilization of this work in whole or in part in any form by any
electronic, mechanical or other means, now known or hereafter
invented, including xerography, photocopying and recording, or in
any information storage or retrieval system, is forbidden without
the written permission of the editorial office, Silhouette Books,
233 Broadway, New York, NY 10279 U.S.A.

All characters in this book have no existence outside the imagination of
the author and have no relation whatsoever to anyone bearing the same
name or names. They are not even distantly inspired by any individual
known or unknown to the author, and all incidents are pure invention.

This edition published by arrangement with Harlequin Books S.A.

® and TM are trademarks of Harlequin Books S.A., used under license.
Trademarks indicated with ® are registered in the United States Patent
and Trademark Office, the Canadian Trade Marks Office and in other
countries.

Visit Silhouette at www.eHarlequin.com

Printed in U.S.A.

Books by Kate Welsh

Silhouette Special Edition

Substitute Daddy #1542

Steeple Hill Love Inspired

For the Sake of Her Child #39
Never Lie to an Angel #69
A Family for Christmas #83
Small-Town Dreams #100
Their Forever Love #120
*The Girl Next Door #156
*Silver Lining #173
*Mountain Laurel #187
*Her Perfect Match #196

*Laurel Glen

KATE WELSH,

a lover of all things romantic, has been writing romance for nearly twenty years. She is a three-time finalist and two-time winner of Romance Writers of America's coveted Golden Heart and was a RITA® Award finalist in 2000. *Substitute Daddy* is her first Silhouette Special Edition novel but her tenth published novel.

Kate lives just outside Philadelphia in Havertown, Pennsylvania, with her husband of over thirty years, her daughter and her Chesapeake Bay retriever, Ecko. And Kali the family cat, who didn't want a playmate when the puppy moved in two years ago and still doesn't!

Dear Reader,

Every once in a while a scene comes into my head, and if I am lucky a book evolves. The prologue of this book was just such a moment for me and *Substitute Daddy* was just such a book. I'm so excited to have had such a magical experience evolve into my first book for Silhouette Special Edition.

As a writer I do a lot of "what if" thinking. I don't think there is a better way to enrich a story than to insert a few dire "what ifs" to an interesting scene. So I set about upping the heroine's conflict and added a hero from the other side of the fence. I made him a man in transition and gave him a lot to lose and learn and a lot of love to give.

And *Substitute Daddy* was born. I hope you enjoy reading it as much as I enjoyed writing it.

Kate Welsh

R02007 53493

Prologue

The sky was crying, Melissa Abell thought looking
out the window of the funeral parlor. As far as she
was concerned, that was the only explanation for the
constant downpour of the past few days. A light had
gone out of the world and it was in mourning. That
light was her vibrant twin sister Leigh and the love
Leigh had shared with her husband Gary. Gone. Both
gone.

Melissa's gaze was drawn once again to the closed
oak caskets that held all that was left of Leigh and
Gary. She was grateful for those closed coffins. This
way she'd remember both of them the way they'd
looked when she'd last seen them, happily planning a
nursery. She put her hand on her still-flat stomach—
a nursery for the baby she still carried for them.

Melissa looked around at the tasteful room and its
profusion of flowers. She should thank Gary's brother

when he arrived for the thoughtfulness of the arrangements.

And she would.

Even if it killed her.

Gary's immediate family were conspicuous by their absence. She had already stood alone by the caskets for two hours, greeting and accepting condolences from other Costain family members and Gary and Leigh's friends and acquaintances. As she checked her watch, Melissa heard a commotion at the door. Gary's brother and parents had finally arrived—just short of the time the service was set to begin. In at least this, she knew his brother, Brett, was innocent. No two brothers had ever been closer.

Melissa waited until they'd gotten their raincoats off and were ready to parade into the room, then she walked to her seat and signaled the minister to begin the service. If that left the Costains scrambling into the first row, so be it.

What kind of people were late for their own son's funeral?

The minister, a kindly man who'd been Melissa's support these last two difficult hours, stood at her cue. He clearly understood her feelings. If the Costains had wanted to honor their son, they'd have been on time. They could accept condolences later.

The minister prayed for Gary and Leigh, then called on the mourners to celebrate their short lives rather than spend time dwelling on their tragic passing. He mentioned Brett's loss of his best friend and brother and the Costains' loss of a son. He spoke of Melissa's own tearing loss of a twin and urged her to cherish the special bond she'd shared with Leigh and Gary. It was unnecessary to tell her to remember that bond, considering she carried Gary's child, but Melissa appreciated the sentiment just the same.

Before she realized it, the kindly man was leading them in the Lord's Prayer and the service had ended. Since Leigh and Gary were to be cremated and the ashes interred in the Costain family vault at a later time, they were all spared a rainy scene at the cemetery.

The funeral director stepped to the minister's side and invited everyone to a luncheon at Bellfield. He didn't even find it necessary to say it was the Costains' estate or to give directions. They were just all expected to know what he meant and where it was. She supposed anyone who didn't know wasn't welcome.

Melissa dismissed her annoyance with a shake of her head. Whether or not she was welcome didn't matter anyway because she had no intention of attending. Or inhabiting their rarefied world one second longer than necessary.

By the time they all sat down to soup, she would probably be in Delaware—well on the road toward home. Back where she came from. Back to where she belonged.

Melissa had just stooped down to pick up her purse when two highly-polished, black, Italian loafers stepped into view. Brett. Steeling herself and fighting for calm with every fiber of her being, she stood to confront Gary's brother. Still handsome as the devil she knew him to be, his black hair was combed off his face and still wet from the downpour. His pale gray eyes as carefully blanked as they'd been the last time she saw him at Leigh and Gary's wedding.

His face was a mask of decorum, so different from

the oh-so-sexy charmer he'd been the night before Leigh and Gary were married.

"The service turned out well," he said, as if searching for a neutral topic.

"Yes. It did. Thank you for arranging everything so nicely. It was lovely."

He nodded. "I'm sorry we were so late. My parents' plane was held up. They decided not to fly home until this morning."

Was his annoyance directed at his parents, the airline or her for signaling the start of the service the way she had? Melissa realized she really didn't care.

"It was a lovely service anyway. I'm sure everyone will have time to express their condolences to your family at the luncheon," Melissa said, wishing he would just go away.

"Would you like to ride to the estate with us?"

"I have my car," she answered. It wasn't a lie. She *did* have her car. It just happened to be parked around the corner, packed with her clothes and the few personal things she'd wanted as remembrances of Leigh and Gary. The bank and Gary's family could divvy up what little was left. Since Gary had recently gone out on his own to start a management consulting business, he hadn't built up much equity in his company yet. And she certainly didn't want to prolong her association with the Costains by demanding anything for the baby. As far as she was concerned, she was ready to hit the road and leave Pennsylvania behind.

"I wanted to get together with you about your plans for the baby," Brett said. "I thought after the luncheon we would be able to speak privately. It shouldn't take long."

"Of course," she said in a noncommittal tone. Her

plans? Considering the kind of people the Costains were, she hadn't thought any of them would care. But it didn't matter. She had no obligation to the parents who had made Gary's life so miserable. What she'd heard of his childhood appalled her. There was no way she would expose her precious child to people who were as cold and self-centered as the Costains.

Brett stepped back and gave her a sharp nod. "Fine. We'll talk later at Bellfield then."

We'll talk later all right. Much later. Like when hell freezes over, Melissa thought as Brett turned away and went to stand with his mother. Moments later, as they filed out of the room, she said a mental goodbye to the entire Costain clan. Frightening as it was, she was on her own.

Her baby was an Abell now.

Chapter One

Brett turned left on Route 5 in Hughesville, Maryland. Tired from the long drive after several exhausting and frustrating weeks, he glanced at his directions then back to the road, ready now for the next turn. It had taken two months to track Melissa Abell, but the detective he'd hired through his law firm, Joe Brennan, had finally succeeded. Brennan had determined her address through notice of an inheritance left to her by her uncle. In a few more minutes Brett would, at long last, get the opportunity to confront her and to find out why she'd disappeared.

She'd clearly had plans that hadn't included attending the funeral luncheon. Why not just say so? He'd wanted to offer help with the baby. A baby who was all that was left of his brother—the only person he had ever loved. Why go to so much trouble to deprive him of doing the one thing he could do? Be of financial help.

It made no sense. Melissa wasn't prepared for single parenthood. She was only pregnant because she'd generously agreed to have Gary's baby through artificial insemination after Leigh learned she was sterile because of an infection.

He fought the excess emotion he always felt whenever he thought of Melissa. They'd met at Bellfield the night before Gary and Leigh's wedding. In town for the nuptials, Melissa had appeared to be every bit as sophisticated and cosmopolitan as her twin sister— a facade he hadn't seen through in time.

By the time he'd held her in his arms on the dance floor, his fate had been sealed, and by the time the music changed beats, he'd wanted a lot more than dancing. Like her under him and them holding each other as close as two people can get.

Dancing soon led to a midnight walk in the gardens and a hot and heavy interlude in the pool house. If she hadn't made a frustratingly naive comment, he would have taken her virginity then and there. But trepidation and near panic had flooded him, making him pause. Forcing him to think.

That moment had been the low point of his life because in a blinding flash he'd come face-to-face with the truth about himself. There in the pool house, on what had been the most magical night of his life, he'd come crashing back to reality. Virginity inherently meant some kind of deep commitment and he was lousy at deep and commitment. Too much like his father they all said. He'd been told so by enough women, his mother included, and it had finally sunk in.

He'd calmed things down quickly then, and he and Melissa returned to the party, which by that time had been breaking up. Troubled, he'd slept little that night. No woman had ever made him feel the way she had, and he'd been afraid he wouldn't be able to resist her again. Since Brett knew he'd eventually hurt Melissa terribly once she understood the kind of man he was, it was a given that their inevitable breakup would harm his relationship with Gary or at the very least, complicate Gary's life.

So Brett had decided to be charming and friendly to Melissa at the wedding but to make himself scarce around her. That plan had gone by the boards when she'd walked down the aisle ahead of her sister. He'd nearly been knocked flat by the uncontrollable yearning to hold her again.

Still hurting over his epiphany the night before and the vision of the lonely future it had given him, he'd doubted his self-control around Melissa even more. Determined to thwart his own runaway emotions, Brett decided to enlist the help of an old family friend to use as a buffer between him and Melissa. He hadn't counted on Melissa being hurt and angry so early in their non-relationship when she'd seen him with someone else, but he'd decided the damage was done and had let things stand—not trusting himself to go to her and explain.

Now, five years later, because she'd practically fled the city two months ago after the funeral service, he had to meet with her in private without the protection of fellow mourners as he'd planned. The prospect had his heart pounding as he drew closer to her home.

He was afraid—very much afraid—he was just as attracted to the pretty, sweet look of her now as he had been to her glamorous alter ego five long years ago. And he didn't like it.

Not one bit.

Brett spotted his next turn and was soon flying along a winding road into the middle of nowhere. He passed one Amish farm after another, and several other properties in much poorer condition than their non-electrified Amish neighbors.

He had to go around several slow-moving horse-drawn buggies driven by bearded men in flat-crowned hats. For some odd reason the children peering out of the back windows took great pleasure in waving to him. It was just too hard to ignore their shining faces. He didn't have a great deal of experience where children were concerned, but it felt wrong not to smile just as broadly and wave back.

Several miles farther along, when his frustration level reached a new high and his annoyance at his own trepidation over this meeting was right up there with it, he saw a listing, rusted mailbox. He brought the car to a screeching halt, kicking up a storm of dust in the gravel at the end of a long crushed-stone drive. Ancient, faded letters on the side of the box spelled out Abell.

He looked up the drive through the dark tunnel of trees and saw nothing but shadows. But she was there. He knew it. His search was over. He'd found her. And his brother's child.

Trying to bury his feelings and hang on to the anger over all the trouble she'd put him through, Brett headed his sturdy little sports car into the rutted stone drive. After a sharp bend in the road, the tunnel of trees surrounding the vehicle abruptly ended.

Several smallish, broken-down barns and a clapboard farmhouse that had seen better days sat in the middle of the clearing. In the background were acres of grass and weeds bisected with weathered white-washed fencing. The house and farm buildings were screened from the road by the thick trees and scrub that had been flying by his window minutes before.

He turned his attention back to the house and frowned. More than half of the white paint had peeled to bare, weathered wood and several of its forest-green shutters were missing. On the front porch, two wicker chairs rocked languidly in the warm early-summer breeze. A rainbow of flowers blooming along the foundation of the porch brightened the dismal setting, but only a little.

Brett pushed open his door and climbed to his feet. He looked around, unable to connect this place with the woman he'd been tracking. Or at least his image of her. Had everything she said been a lie? This did not look like the house of a decorator.

Now that he thought about it, if, indeed, she'd been an interior designer with a business of her own and plans for an antique shop, as she'd said at the wedding, how could she have left all that behind five years later to stay with Gary and Leigh in their spare room until the baby was born? That kind of absence would be death to a business.

And if all that was a lie too, how did she expect to support a child? The detective's report had said the place was run-down, but that it would be worth good money to a developer. It also said she had made no move to sell so that clearly wasn't part of her plan. What the report or his detective hadn't warned him of was that she was impoverished.

Brett stood there appalled, his anger growing. This

was where Melissa planned to raise Gary's baby? He pictured a barefoot child who looked like Gary, wearing tattered clothes, crouched by the side of the road watching the world go by without him. And shuddered.

What advantage would the child have living in poverty in the back of beyond? Even having him as a guardian would be better than this! He could hire a nanny to provide the everyday security a child needed and he'd make sure to be there for the big moments whenever possible.

Straightening his shoulders, Brett walked forward, prepared to do battle for his brother's son. He'd just put his foot on the bottom step when Melissa spoke through the sagging screen door. "What do you want?" she demanded, her tone hostile.

He took a deep breath. "You skipped lunch," he quipped, striving to keep this meeting as friendly as possible. He was a man on a mission with a child's well-being at stake and alienating the child's mother wouldn't help matters. And he couldn't let his brother's child be brought up this way.

"I had nothing more to say to you or your family," she answered. Her expression was calm. Almost serene. "'Doing lunch' would have been overkill."

Brett arched an eyebrow. "Is that why you ran? Because you had nothing to say?"

"I didn't run. I drove home. It's a free country," she said, still annoyingly composed though no less unfriendly.

He took another calming breath. "We need to talk," he reiterated.

"Oh? What could we possibly have to talk about?"

She pushed open the rickety screen door and stepped onto the porch.

She was still delicate and thin, the pregnancy not showing at all. Her blue-green eyes flashed with anger. He fought a smile that tugged at his lips. She might be angry and sound tough, but with her blond hair curling loosely about her lovely heart-shaped face and the soft material of her light-blue dress fluttering around her calves she looked sweet and innocent. And seductive as hell.

What the hell's the matter with you?

"Look, what I have to say won't take long," he said, forcing his thoughts back on track. "Gary's baby is all I have left of my brother. I have a proposition. Come back to Pennsylvania and live in the carriage house on the estate. It's an attractive little place. Warm. Clean. After the baby's born, if you sign over custody, I'll set you up in business in any city of your choice. You could even have standard visitation rights. It's your smartest way out of the jam Gary and Leigh's deaths have left you in."

Melissa blinked, her mouth a silent O, then suddenly her blue eyes shot sparks and the words came out in a torrent. "And I thought my *first* encounter with you left a lingering bad taste." She took a step forward. "You will never get my baby, Brett Costain. Do you understand?"

"We're talking about a lot of money. And a lot of responsibility off your shoulders."

"A baby is not a *responsibility*. It is not a *jam*. A baby is a cherished gift."

Brett felt the heat of his emotions rise as words tumbled out of his mouth. "I'll go as high as

$100,000. That's the best deal you'll get and you know it.''

"Deal? Money? That's all your family cares about, isn't it? I'd heard the tales from Leigh and Gary all these years but I had no idea how—'' She broke off and shook her head looking terribly, terribly sad. Her teeth clamped on her bottom lip, and she turned her head to stare out over the barren fields. "Your family hurt Gary for years. And Leigh…'' Her sister's name was a broken sigh on the summer breeze. "Go away!''

"Look, Melissa—''

"No. You look. I want you to leave. Now! I went to high school with Sheriff Long. He's a good friend. I think he'd take my word that you're trespassing. This is *my* baby now and no Costain is getting their mercenary hands on my child.''

"Not if a judge decides otherwise,'' he countered, all thought of equitable settlements blasted away by fear for Gary's child.

Melissa's eyes widened then narrowed. Her voice now held no sadness, only rage. "If you aren't off this property in two minutes, I'm calling Hunter Long. That would give you about twenty minutes to get out of this county with him hot on your tail. The clock's ticking. If you tangle with Hunter Long, your name and money won't help you a bit. Have a nice day.''

She turned regally, her skirt swishing seductively, walked inside and slammed the heavy front door, rattling every window in the dilapidated house. Brett stalked back to his BMW roadster and threw himself behind the wheel. He wasn't in the mood to tangle with a county mountie on the warpath so he turned his car around and drove out to the main road. Once there, he pulled to a stop, needing a moment to collect his thoughts.

He'd come here to ask for the occasional visit with the child. But after seeing the way she lived, there was no way he could have left it at that. The only thing that *was* clear was that he wasn't going to get Gary's baby without a fight.

Brett blinked. Get the baby? A fight? What the hell had he said? What the hell had he done?

Chapter Two

About an hour after Brett left, Melissa heard the jingle of a horse's harness and the rattle of Izaak Abramson's wagon. She put down the old coffee grinder she'd just brought up from the cellar and walked out on the porch, promising herself time to clean it up and admire it later.

She waved a greeting.

"Good day to you, Miss Missy," Izaak called. "I have some time today to look at your barn."

What good news! Smiling at Izaak's childhood nickname for her, Melissa skipped down the steps toward the man wearing the same kind of plain black pants and gray shirt he always wore. With Izaak there were rarely surprises.

"Then it's okay?" she sighed, hardly believing at least one of her worries was over.

Izaak nodded. "Margaret spoke to the elders and

explained about the baby. We are all still allowed to be friends and we may still work with you on your shop. They don't like English science but understand that you are not immoral. Just misguided.''

Melissa ignored her annoyance at his last statement and breathed a sigh of relief. It was going to work out. Only now could she admit to herself that she'd been terribly worried. There was no telling how Izaak and Margaret's elders might have reacted to Melissa's impending single motherhood—no matter how impersonally it had come about.

''I'm hoping there's a way to have the barn ready by the time the baby's born. It would be so much better to be able to open the shop close to home and not have it actually in the house.''

Izaak sighed and shook his head. ''You should not need to support yourself. It is the English way to have a child with no father to guide him.''

His disapproval hurt but she straightened her spine. ''Now, Izaak, I know Margaret explained to you that this was supposed to be Leigh and Gary's baby and that I was supposed to act as its aunt.''

Melissa had known Izaak Abramson her whole life. His parents' farm bordered her uncle's, and when she was young, he'd been the object of her dreams. Back then he'd been a handsome, smiling young man who gave her rides on his horse. When he'd married, Melissa had been crushed. He'd promised to wait for her, after all. But her five-year-old heart had healed quickly with a few hugs and attention from Margaret, the love of his life.

Izaak sighed. ''Yes and I know the baby is of English science. But it will be Leigh's baby no longer and the father is not here to help you raise him either.''

His concern touched her and Melissa felt tears once again well up in her eyes. ''No. Neither of them are here, are they?''

Izaak shook his head and clumsily patted her shoulder. ''I've made you sad again. So suppose we look at this barn you have decided to make into a store. Now what is this name we will have on this barn that is no longer to be just a barn?''

She smiled. Izaak had always made her smile. ''Stony Hollow Country and Classics and you know it. It'll be a great partnership. You, me and Margaret.''

And it would be. She had the knowledge of antiques and had been collecting them for the day when her dream came true. She also had the wood. Two falling-down barns' worth! Izaak Abramson had the know-how to turn that weathered wood into furniture. The country movement in decorating had turned old-barn-wood furniture into a valuable commodity and Melissa and Izaak were going to cash in on it. And Margaret's quilting was simply gorgeous. Melissa would feature beautifully displayed Amish quilts—another sought-after product. And there was the quarter-sawn oak furniture Izaak and his brother Od painstakingly built too. They wouldn't get wealthy, but that wasn't the purpose. A good life was.

And she was going to give her child just that. She wouldn't let Brett Costain and his threats make her believe anything else. She'd nearly collapsed when she'd seen him on her porch, but she'd reached inside herself and had faced down one of the supreme Costains. She would do the same in court if it came to that. She would have to.

Melissa could hardly believe she'd stood on her porch, looking down her nose at him, and ordered him off her land. It gave her a little thrill that it had worked so easily. And so well. He was gone—tail tucked between his legs, driving hell-bent-for-leather toward Philadelphia. He was gone.

Gone but not forgotten, a small voice inside her protested.

Okay. He'd hurt her once. She could admit that. She'd seen him as her irreverent, charming knight on a white charger. She'd gotten all caught up in Leigh's fairy-tale wishes for her. And she'd been a fool. They both had.

Leigh had been waxing poetic about Gary's perfect younger brother for weeks. He was funny, kind, handsome as sin and twice as wealthy. He was supposed to have been perfect for Melissa. And she had actually gotten her hopes up when she'd seen the way Brett looked at Leigh and Gary. She could have sworn she saw a deep yearning in his eyes for what they'd found together. Then he'd been all smiles and loving hugs for his aunts and cousins while making Melissa feel like part of the family. *Handsome* had been so great an understatement that Melissa had planned to tease Leigh over it later.

She and Leigh were dressed alike for the first time since their parents died. Leigh had bought the dresses, done Melissa's hair and makeup so they could have fooled even Gary himself. But, of course, it had been Gary's plan. He'd wanted to mislead his parents, who believed Leigh had been raised in the lap of luxury, not on a beaten-down farm in southern Maryland. He'd assured Melissa that proper breeding would matter to them.

Melissa had thought she'd feel self-conscious all dressed up in a sophisticated costume. But it had been worse than that. Leigh and Gary had been wrong to hide the truth and so had Melissa. Wrong to think she could pretend to be someone and something she wasn't. Wrong to get so caught up in the excitement of the game that she forgot some games come with penalties and consequences.

Melissa shook herself from her reverie. What was she doing, thinking about that whole humiliating episode? It had been a long time ago and she was older now and much, much wiser. It was time to think of the future. And as she and Izaak planned the renovations, the future began to look bright again. She refused to think about the shadow on the horizon called Brett Costain.

The old swing creaked as Melissa rocked in the shade of the big "Johnny Smoker" tree off to the left of the house. She smiled at the Philadelphia nickname and reminded herself for the umpteenth time to find out the real name for her favorite tree on the property. She looked up into the boughs as the evening breeze ruffled the big leaves, creating the sound Aunt Dora had always called the song of summer.

Melissa's stomach growled, reminding her that it was dinnertime and of the astounding sensation that had awakened her that morning. Her baby had moved, and for the first time she'd felt a little flutter of life. Her first reaction had been to call Leigh—but then she'd remembered.

She was alone. Completely alone, with all the responsibility that bringing a precious life into the world entailed. She had to secure the baby's future and guard its present.

She was alone. Alone to face the unknown in the form of pregnancy and labor and delivery.

She was alone. Alone to see first smiles, hear first laughter and worry and thrill over first steps.

She'd been close—so close—to calling Hunter and telling him she'd changed her mind. That marriage to a friend was better than going forward alone. But she hadn't called. A good and generous man like Hunter Long deserved a wife who not only loved him but who was *in* love with him and who desired him as well. She'd caught a brief glimpse of those feelings one magical night and even though the object of her affection hadn't returned her feelings she knew what was missing with and from her old friend.

It was ironic that only hours later Brett—the man who'd inadvertently taught her so much—had swept back into her life to teach her another truth. In threatening to take her baby away just as it had become real and not a little frightening to her, he had revealed to her just how precious this baby was.

She sighed and sank a little deeper into the swing. Today had been a very long day.

It had started early with the joy of new life. Fear had come upon her, and then Brett had arrived and drawn anger bursting from the depth of her being. But then Izaak had come by, full of good news and support.

Because his elders had approved their venture, Izaak and his brothers and cousins would be allowed to convert the barn nearest the road and dismantle the others. He had carefully inspected the building and had declared it strong and sound. They had paced off and marked an office and rest room in the loft area, deciding to leave an open-floor plan on the ground floor because it would be more flexible in the future. They decided to add a staircase and a balcony railing at the front of the loft for the display of Margaret Abramson's quilts.

Izaak was so proud of his wife's skilled artistry that Melissa had felt a little surge of the old childhood jealousy. And she'd teased him about it. But he had patted her hand, his mood serious, and told her that God would send a man for her and her baby.

This time he didn't mention Hunter, for which she was grateful. He understood that while she and Hunter could build a family for the baby, they could not build a life on friendship alone.

She sighed again, regretful but resigned. At least this way she'd have the home and child she'd always dreamed of to soften the loss of Leigh.

She closed her eyes, reaching inside herself for the memory of Leigh's bright laughter and her wide smile. She relived the wonderful scene the day Melissa's pregnancy had been confirmed. She and Leigh had both been waiting in the couple's living room when Gary got home. Leigh had given him a silly T-shirt about fatherhood. Gary had stared down at it for a long moment then let out a joy-filled whoop before lifting Leigh in the air and spinning her around. When he'd put Leigh down, he rushed to Melissa and engulfed her in a bear hug, thanking her with grateful tears in his eyes.

The sound of an engine and the crunch of gravel disrupted summer's song and Leigh and Gary slipped silently back into Melissa's memory. She wiped away her tears and stood, then walked around the side of the porch and froze. It appeared the day would end the way it had begun—with the annoyance of Brett Costain.

Melissa stalked forward to meet him, studiously ignoring the way the sun glinted off his blue-black hair. "Did you think I was kidding about calling Hunter Long?"

"No. But I thought talking to you again and settling things more amicably would be worth the risk."

"And I told you we have nothing to talk about."

"Which is my fault. I shot my mouth off. My only excuse is that all of this threw me more than just a little." He gestured to the house and surrounding buildings. "You have to admit this is pretty far removed from the world I was raised in."

Melissa looked around and tried to see the scene from his point of view. Gary and Leigh's four-bedroom colonial had been far removed from his upbringing. She supposed her house, scraped and not yet painted, with its broken shutters not back from being repaired, looked rather shabby. Add two barns whose only virtue could be found in their salvage value, and she could guess what he thought. But that was no excuse for the way he'd acted or the things he'd threatened.

"This is my home. It will be my child's home. This isn't Philadelphia. It isn't Devon. This is St. Marys County, Maryland, where a lot of people are poor. No judge is going to take away my baby because my house needs painting and repairs."

"And neither would I," he said quickly. "I'm sorry about the threat. I wasn't out of your driveway before I realized what I'd said. I didn't come here this morning to upset you or threaten you. I came for answers.

And to offer help. Now that I see your situation I can see you need it.''

She'd meant what she said about the judge and the courts but his reappearance was still upsetting. No mother took his kind of threat lightly, especially considering the things she knew about his family. But that wasn't why her legs were shaking and her heart was pounding in her chest.

It was him.

Melissa didn't know why his nearness always affected her like this. It was the same now when she was angry with him as it had been five years ago when all she'd wanted was to feel his lips on hers.

Knowing it would be stupid to antagonize him by again asking him to leave, and needing desperately to sit, Melissa gestured toward the porch. ''I don't want your help but I'll see what I can do about those answers you mentioned.'' She turned and walked up the steps, sinking gratefully into one of the big wicker rockers, the one Uncle Ed used to sit in for hours. She could almost feel his comforting presence surround her.

Brett followed and pulled the mate to her chair so it faced hers more directly. He leaned forward, propped his elbows on his knees and laced the long fingers of his beautiful hands. He was such an incredibly handsome man. No wonder women nearly swooned at his feet—the rat.

''I needed to know why you lied to me,'' the rat asked.

Melissa sat back in the chair and crossed her arms, pinning him with a hostile glare. ''I told you, I didn't lie. I left. My stay with Gary and Leigh was temporary. I was under no obligation to walk in the front door of Bellfield again or to remain in Pennsylvania. But you know all that.''

''No. That isn't what I mean. I'm talking about the lie five years ago when you almost destroyed my relationship with my brother.''

She could feel and hear his suppressed anger. The fingers which had looked graceful and relaxed only moments ago were now clenched tightly. Had she nearly come between the brothers? It had never been her intention. Had Leigh not felt her pain and anger at the wedding reception, Melissa would never have told her sister what had happened with Brett.

Melissa told Brett all of that now, adding, ''But I don't understand how you think I lied to you.''

''You aren't the same person. This you is the real you. The person I met shouldn't have been so upset when one night was all I could offer. She wouldn't have been hurt because our stolen moments in the pool house weren't about happily ever after. The person I met lived in the real world, not the back of beyond with rocking chairs and porches and barns. She was a designer. She had plans to open an antique store. She was glamorous and worldly and cosmopolitan. *She* wasn't you.''

Melissa nodded, seeing for the first time that Brett hadn't been unaffected by that night or the masquerade. ''Oh what a tangled web we weave...'' she thought.

''The way I was dressed was the facade. One Leigh and Gary created. It shouldn't have been necessary, but, because all your family cares about are appearances and bank accounts, it was necessary for Gary. He was sure they'd use Leigh's upbringing after our parents died as a new source of ridicule. He didn't want the love of his life used as a weapon against him. He knew it would hurt her. Leigh and I knew it would hurt him. And Gary had been hurt enough.''

Brett sat back in his chair slowly, taking the words in, thinking about them solemnly. "I agree and I understand what and who prompted it. They're my parents too. But Gary lied to me. Then he was furious with me for treating you like the person you pretended to be without bothering to tell me you'd been playing dress up.''

She could see beyond his anger to the hurt in his light-gray eyes. They were filled with pain.

"What I don't understand—" he continued "—is why he kept it from *me*. We didn't keep secrets from each other. Why do you think I'm the only one who knows for sure that there's a baby on the way?"

Melissa leaned back in her chair also, letting her face rest in the shadows as she spoke. "He said the two of you were always having to keep secrets from your parents. He wanted to let you off the hook with this one. That's all it was, Brett. His commitment to Leigh was a lifetime one. If Gary had told you, he felt he would be forcing you to keep his secret for just as long. We'd originally come up with a scenario in which I would pretend to move to the farm I'd inherited from a distant relative. I was going to say I enjoyed the area and had decided to stay. Since it turned out that I preferred not to visit when you'd be around, he decided updating you and your parents with the story no longer mattered.''

Brett pursed his lips and nodded, then looked off, staring at the barn closest to the house. "I would never have touched you if I'd known the truth. I wish to God he'd told me.''

"Well, you aren't the only one," she snapped. She still smarted from his incredulous look when she'd found him in the arms of another woman not twenty-four hours after he'd held her, kissing her in the same way. He'd so dazzled her that she'd almost compromised her principles for him. And that had hurt.

"I didn't mean to hurt you," he said quietly.

Melissa hated that he saw the truth. "Don't flatter yourself. You infuriated me. That's all there was to it," she lied.

"I didn't mean to do that either," Brett said, his voice solemn. "But I *know* I hurt you. I saw your tears before you turned away. Plus Gary had a lot to say on the subject." He grimaced. "And I'm sorry, but I *was* misinformed."

"Only about my clothing. I'm not a country bumpkin just because intimacy means something to me."

He nodded. "Fine. I think, considering present circumstances, it's time we bury the hatchet somewhere other than in each other's backs."

She hoped she would never see him again so what did it matter? Forgiving him wouldn't change anything but there was something to be said for a lack of enemies. Melissa nodded.

Brett sighed, clearly relieved. "Now, about help."

Melissa stood. "I don't want your money. Money comes with strings and I don't want anything tying us to your family."

She realized her error when he looked up at her, his hair stirring in the breeze. Standing had put her in closer proximity to him. He was too damn handsome by half. She sat back down, hating that his nearness could still affect her.

"I didn't say anything about strings or conditions," he said softly. "I offered help."

"Charity always has conditions, Brett. And there's another thing about money you don't seem to understand. Money doesn't fix your threat. Money doesn't buy trust. I accepted your apology for the way you treated me at the wedding because I think it was sincerely given, but I haven't forgiven your threat to me or my child's happiness. And I won't, because money also doesn't buy forgiveness."

Chapter Three

Stung by the truth of what Melissa had said, Brett nodded, ready to leave for the time being, but determined to find some other way to reach her. He refused to do it with legal threats or by scaring her with the very real worry that his mother could turn out to be a threat all her own.

Still he had to do something. He couldn't let it go at this. Maybe he'd been a lawyer too long. Maybe, as Melissa said, he'd been a Costain too long. "For what it's worth, I'm sorry I frightened you. I only came here to offer help. There should be a little left in Gary's estate, and his child is entitled to it. I'll be in touch." He sighed and stood, grappling to say the right thing. Instead he settled for neutrality. "In the meantime, take care of yourself until I see you again."

He turned away and left her there on the porch. He looked back at her before climbing into his car. She looked like the heroine of an old movie. Sitting in a rocker on the porch of the dilapidated farmhouse with the breeze ruffling her fine golden hair so it shimmered in the dying sunlight, she was too beautiful for words.

Hesitating, Brett fingered his keys before starting his car, forcing his mind into numbness. It was only when he turned onto Route 5 again, that he remembered passing a shopping center with a rather large grocery store. Food was something everyone needed. And what was the old saying? She was eating for two now. If he bought her groceries, he'd help the baby in the only way he could right then, and he'd help Melissa because she could spend what little money she had on other things.

So he found a motel out on the highway, and the next morning at 6:00 a.m., Brett entered a supermarket for the first time in years. It was his housekeeper's job to keep his cupboards stocked and he hadn't remembered how much fun food shopping could be. He went up and down the aisles filling the cart to overflowing with everything that looked healthy or useful. Soon it was full, but he'd saved the most important aisle for last. It was the one aimed exclusively toward the needs and wants of babies and small children.

He went down there to remind himself why he was there in the first place. Then the cutest brown bear caught his eye. He picked it up and decided it must be too early in the morning for rational thought. He could have sworn the look in the little guy's soft golden eyes begged for a home. He put it back on the shelf, but its soft fur caressed his fingertips as he drew them away and its head sort of flopped sadly to the side.

He might have managed to walk away but he remembered Gary buying several toys in the two weeks he'd known about the baby. Gary wouldn't have put the bear back, so Brett added it to the cart then hustled back to the card aisle. He picked out a gift bag and a matching note card, then headed for the checkout.

Once he returned to the car with sacks and sacks of food and other essentials, Brett wrote a note saying he would be back for a brief visit. He longed to say something else, anything else, but what could he say that would fix the muddle he'd caused with his runaway emotions and tongue the previous day?

Not wanting to spark another confrontation with Melissa, he coasted the last several yards of the drive with the engine off. Then he quietly began transferring the bags from his trunk to her porch. Once done, he returned to his car, turned it on, and got the hell out of Dodge before she sicced her friend the sheriff on him.

The farther he got from Melissa, though, the more thoughts of her haunted him. It didn't feel right leaving her destitute to face bringing a child into the world. Especially when it was his brother's child, and being kindhearted had gotten her into this fix. He had to find a way to get her to accept financial help.

She didn't want strings to his family. He could understand that. His parents, aunts, uncles and cousins had continually treated Gary and Leigh with disdain. And Leigh, who had been hungry for family after losing her own, had been hurt almost as much as his brother by their contempt. No wonder Melissa wanted so desperately to protect the baby she carried from his family.

He had to admit he did as well, or he'd have told

his parents that Melissa had conceived Gary's baby in the procedure performed a month before his death. His mother hadn't asked. She had merely wondered aloud if she'd have to do something drastic to assure the possible grandchild was brought up properly.

Brett had kept his mouth shut and hadn't questioned what she'd meant before she'd resumed her trip following the funeral. In his heart, though, he knew the answer. His mother would sue for custody in a New York minute if she saw the way Melissa lived.

Melissa opened her front door on her way to get her Sunday *Washington Post* and couldn't believe her eyes. No less than twenty grocery bags and one small gift bag sat at the edge of the porch all lined up like toy soldiers. She walked onto the porch bewildered and stood staring down at the bounty. There were three bags half-full of fresh produce alone!

But then the bewilderment started dissolving like dew on a summer morning. Half-full? They were all half-full. As if they'd purposely been loaded lightly. As if someone hadn't wanted her carrying anything too heavy. Which meant they were from someone who knew about the baby. It wouldn't be Izaak or Margaret or anyone from the Amish community. They brought meals in baskets and would never just leave them. Hunter thought the drive-in at the new fast-food franchise was the modern way to food shop.

It had to be Brett!

Brett.

Of the people she knew, he was the only one extravagant enough to leave all of this just sitting on someone's porch in the hope that it would be accepted. Hadn't he listened to a thing she said? He was still trying to buy his way into her baby's life. She had a mind to let it sit there to rot in the hot sun!

Then she saw a patch of curly brown fur peeking out of the cloud-and-rainbow gift bag and couldn't resist the temptation. Stuffed animals were her one weakness in life—she refused to count the light-headed effect Brett had on her.

Melissa reluctantly bent down and pulled out a soft, floppy brown bear. She might have been able to ignore a beseeching expression in Brett's striking gray eyes but not in the bear's golden ones.

She tried all day to tell herself she'd been nothing but practical to bring the groceries into the kitchen and put them away. After all, she couldn't really leave all that food to rot on her porch. It would draw every bit of wildlife on the property to her front door and create a mess she'd have to clean up later, she rationalized. And grocery shopping was such a chore. Her days were busy with rebuilding her business and hunting down stock for the shop. It would have been foolish to let the food go to waste.

Ultimately, sitting down at the kitchen table, staring at the teddy bear in her hands, Melissa admitted to herself that something in Brett's gesture touched her…once her initial annoyance wore off. And that softening attitude toward him bothered her. Every time she looked up from the decorating sample book she was putting together, the teddy bear's sweet face snagged her attention. Annoyed, she finally smacked her hand on the table and jumped up.

"A leopard doesn't change its spots in a matter of hours. You are not going to fool me, Brett Costain," she declared, and stalked to the bear, intending to put him back in the bag. But something inside the bag tangled with the bear's legs when she tried. That's when she found the envelope she'd overlooked earlier. Frowning, Melissa tore it open.

"'Dear Melissa,'" she read aloud. "'I apologize again for the things I said. I don't wish to intrude on your life but as you're carrying my brother's child there's no way I can withdraw completely. I'll be back next weekend to continue the talk we started. Please take care of yourself. BJC.'"

"BJC. What's the J stand for? Jerk? You show up here again and I'll have Hunter toss you out of the county on your ear," she muttered through clenched teeth, blessedly annoyed at him once again.

Brett pulled into Melissa's long drive the following Saturday at a little after noon. He'd put in a long week of rescheduled meetings and late-night dinners with clients trying to cram six days' worth of work into five. He hoped this visit with Melissa would make it all worthwhile.

He wasn't the least bit surprised when she barreled out the front door before he reached the top step of the porch. "I thought I'd made myself clear," she said, standing with her arms crossed belligerently.

She wore her hostility like a shield, but the effect was destroyed by the flowing, calf-length, white cotton dress she also wore. Her golden hair, a tumble of loose curls glinting in the sunlight, absolutely begged for a man's hands to muss it even more. Her blue eyes practically sparked with indignation, making him long to see them once again hot with arousal instead of irritation.

Will you give it a rest! She can't stand the sight of you, you pathetic jerk.

He sighed and reminded himself that, though she looked good enough to eat, his attraction to her was also illogical and irrelevant. It had to be. He was there to discuss the trust fund he'd set up. Anything else would get in the way. Eyes on the prize, he lectured himself, but his self-control around Melissa was practically nonexistent. He'd proven that to himself and Gary five years ago.

"You made yourself perfectly clear," he told her, closing the car door slowly. "You don't like me. You don't trust me. And you don't forgive me. I have to earn all three. Did I miss anything?" Folding his arms before him, Brett leaned against his car.

"Yes." Melissa rushed toward him, then stopped abruptly, halfway down the weed-laden path. She eyed him cautiously. "Actually you failed to tell me what it is you're up to with these little impromptu visits."

"How can I earn your forgiveness, your trust or your goodwill if we never see each other? I owe it to Gary's child to try."

She huffed out a quick breath. "You are so infuriating. I can't imagine you're interested in a baby, even Gary's baby. They're noisy, demanding, often smelly and they're always there. You can't buy them off with expensive jewelry when they become inconvenient."

Brett felt his cheeks heat. So Leigh had told her that too. "I never thought I could. Nor would I want to. And once again, I'm not trying to maneuver a way to take your baby. Please believe I was speaking from anger and surprise when I said that. I'm not asking for access to the baby for my parents or any other family members. I'm the only one who even knows you are pregnant. I'm asking you to accept a check each month from a trust fund I've set up for Gary's child. I loved my brother and I want his child to have everything he needs to build a successful future. Is that so hard to understand?''

''Well, no.'' Pensively, Melissa turned and walked back to the porch to sit in the rocker where he'd left her last weekend. He followed.

''I guess that's a step in the right direction. But I have to wonder if your definition of a successful life and mine bear any resemblance to each other. What's your definition?''

The answer was so obvious he didn't know why she'd bothered to ask. Brett stared at her. She was serious. He frowned. Maybe his answer was a little too obvious. Why did he suddenly feel as if he'd walked into a minefield? How could so simple a question suddenly take on all the features of a riddle?

He knew his silence screamed indecision, but still he hesitated to give his answer. He just couldn't imagine another possible response than the one that had leapt to his tongue, but he was sure she must be seeking a different sort of reply.

Leaning against the porch railing, Brett tried to look relaxed, while feeling anything but. ''Ideally, I think children should get a good education at the best school that can be provided for them. Then they should finish their education at an Ivy League university or one of the Seven Sisters colleges, again, if at all possible. By then they should be ready to move into a career that will eventually net somewhere in the six-figure range.''

''Education *is* important. I agree.'' Melissa looked up at him as if to emphasize her point. ''But who's to say what makes one school better than another for a particular child?''

"That's the job of a parent to decide. From what I've seen, it's often decided while the child is an infant.''

"Really? Leigh and I went to public school because my aunt and uncle chose to save the money from our parents' estate for college and maybe graduate school.''

"That was a wise decision.''

"After high school Leigh wanted an urban setting and a big school, so she left here to go to the Philadelphia area and went to the University of Pennsylvania. My aunt and uncle advised us and they steered Leigh away from a lesser school in Baltimore.''

"Another good choice. See. Our values aren't all that different.''

She held up her hand. "I said *Leigh*. I stayed here and went to Saint Mary's College. Ever hear of it?''

He shook his head.

"Not many people have. It's a good school. Small. Quiet. Perfect for me. We reached these decisions together. Leigh and I headed in completely opposite directions and to diametrically opposed environments. And we were identical twins.''

But they'd been alike in so many ways. Their feelings toward marriage and family for instance. Yet Brett knew Leigh had loved the hustle and bustle of city life and Melissa was clearly a country girl. Country woman, he amended with slightly clenched jaw. He was still so affected by her that it hurt to look at her knowing if he had been a different sort of man she could have been his. He didn't want it to bother him but he was honest enough with himself to admit that it did.

"You two weren't the same at all, were you?" Brett said, trying to cast aside old regrets.

Melissa shook her head.

"So you're saying that if you couldn't handle attending the same university as your identical twin, a parent would be wrong to unilaterally decide where their child goes based on the school's reputation alone."

"Exactly. And it goes further than that. I know you think money's a deciding factor to a choice of a career, but it isn't the only factor to consider either. In public relations, Leigh would easily have been able to pull down the kind of salary you mentioned." She fingered the soft-looking cotton of her dress, a wistful expression settling on her pretty features. "But she met Gary and he and a life together became more important to her. Leigh cut back on her workload by moving to a smaller, less-prestigious firm. And Gary's whole reason for starting his own business was so he could set his own hours. They were happy.

"I'm in the middle of getting my decorating business up and running again." She pointed to the barn that sat toward the front of the property. "I'm also about to convert that barn over there into the antique shop I once told you I wanted to open. And I'm going to stay right here where I'm happy and raise my baby. I might not set the world on fire financially or the shop and business might blossom beyond my wildest dreams. But whatever happens, I'll consider myself successful if my child has everything it needs, and if I look forward to my days at work when I put my feet on the floor each morning."

Melissa was staring at him when he looked back from a quick glance at the barn. He'd never seen her look more impassioned. Explaining this to him really mattered to her.

She continued, "I always considered Gary extremely successful because he liked what he was doing, and he and Leigh were deliriously happy. That's success, Brett, but your family called him a failure and a fool. By the standards you set a few minutes ago, that's your opinion of him as well."

Brett shook his head and sank into the chair across from hers. Gary hadn't been a failure or a fool. But had Brett treated him like one? He honestly didn't think he had but... Could that be the reason Gary had kept the secret about Leigh's upbringing from him? Brett was a lawyer for God's sake. He kept secrets all the time. Secrets that were a lot more complicated than where and how someone had grown up. Had Gary thought Brett would ridicule Leigh and him?

"Brett? Are you happy?" Melissa asked, calling him back to the issue at hand. "Do you even know what it is to be happy?"

Happy? Brett stared at her, his mind this time devoid of an answer. Apparently, happiness was a concept he wasn't at all familiar with. He wasn't *un*happy. Was he?

Brett shrugged. "I suppose happiness is *one* measure of success," he allowed, however uncertainly.

Melissa shook her head. "No. For me, it's *the* measure. And that's my problem with accepting any money from you. If I take one penny, you'll think you have the right to influence or dictate how I raise my child. I know Gary spent a miserable childhood. I don't know how you felt about it, but he resented the hell out of it.''

Brett just couldn't expose his feelings to her. She unsettled him too much already. Held too much power over him, though she didn't seem to know it. It was difficult to even think straight in her presence. She made him uncomfortable in ways he hadn't felt since discovering R-rated movies in his early teens.

He'd always contended that if he'd known how inexperienced Melissa was the night he'd nearly seduced her, he never would've touched her. He'd consoled himself for years with that claim. But now he wasn't sure. And that was a very scary conclusion because it meant he didn't know himself very well.

He was about to assure Melissa that all he wanted was for her to accept the trust fund, but all at once he knew that would never be enough. Though he was certainly not father material, he couldn't stand the thought of just staying on the fringes of this child's life.

Melissa sat across from him trying to look stern and tough and all the while he could see incredible love for her child shining in her eyes and peeking out of her careful defense of her way of life. He didn't have a clue why he felt all the needs today that had exploded in him five years ago but there was little sense in denying that those feelings raged through him once again. He was drawn to every aspect of her personality he'd been taught to disdain, and he knew he should stay away from her.

But he couldn't be a part of her child's life without her cooperation. And she hated him. Which meant he had to find a way to change her mind. Charm her.

Make her need him. See him as indispensable. That was it! He never failed at that.

His parents needed his help in maintaining Bellfield. The firm needed his growing reputation. Women were never the ones to leave even with all their complaints about his workload and tendency to remain aloof. And that was because he gave them anything they wanted but his heart.

He'd have to control himself where Melissa was concerned while being so helpful and charming she wouldn't be able to imagine her life without him. There was no reason to think he couldn't do both even though at that moment Melissa looked about as pliable as a steel girder.

He needed to develop a strategy, but at least now he had the germ of a plan. He stood to leave and moved the chair back to where he'd found it. "Will you at least think about the advantages the trust fund could give the baby? I promise not to interfere with any value structure you set for your child," he promised.

"I'm not a fool, Brett. I know money isn't necessarily the root of all evil and that it's also a handy tool in the right hands. It isn't the money, but who it comes from that worries me. I don't know if I can trust you to keep your opinions to yourself. I don't want to spend the next eighteen or twenty years policing your influence."

Chapter Four

Someone pounded on Melissa's front door the following Saturday, waking her from a perfectly wonderful dream that Brett starred in. She couldn't help being annoyed at whoever had snatched her from his arms. Then she realized what she was thinking and aimed that stupid anger straight at herself. What was with her and all these ridiculous dreams she'd been having lately? She'd positively gone around the bend!

In her half-awake state, she tossed on her robe and made her way down the steps. When she pulled open the door, she found Brett, but he wasn't pounding on her door. He was standing on the ground at the skirt of the porch pounding on the porch floor from below with a hand sledge, loosening the deteriorating floorboards.

To further befuddle her already disordered brain, he was dressed as she'd never seen him—in worn jeans and a faded T-shirt. And there was more. The muscles of his arms stood out in stark definition beneath his tanned skin. She had never thought of Brett as a particularly physical man but that's the way he looked in the early-morning light.

"What are you doing?" she asked for some reason, even though the answer was obvious. Anything to keep from acknowledging the heat she felt when she looked at him dressed like a man instead of a *GQ* mannequin.

This isn't good, Melissa had enough sense to tell herself. She tried in vain to find that nice liberal dose of anger she'd been feeling only minutes ago. But then Brett looked up and smiled.

"I..." he started to reply, then stopped and just stared. It was as if his powers of speech had abruptly deserted him.

Melissa's heart flipped in her chest when his burning gaze traced her body from her toes to her face. She couldn't move. She couldn't breathe. What she saw in his eyes was more dangerous than all the strings to all the trust funds in the world. She clutched her robe closed with a tighter grip and felt her face heat.

But then his smile mutated into that lady-killer grin of his. Fury flooded her brain. And she was free. Gloriously free.

Melissa didn't say a word but turned and slammed the door behind her. Oh, no. He was *not* going to charm her the way he did his legion of women. He probably thought that was a way into her life with the baby. How could she have forgotten for even one millisecond the kind of man he was?

Again she asked herself, what on earth was the matter with her? First she dreamed of the man, then for a few seconds there she'd actually believed he was looking at her with desire and she'd liked it. She knew all about the swinging door on his bedroom and all the kiss-off gifts he'd given to those women. She herself had already felt the pain of his fickle-hearted rejection.

Her doctor had warned her that her hormones would go haywire, but she hadn't thought he meant she'd lose all reason! She'd dreamed of Brett this week and, instead of waking annoyed, she woke feeling needy. It had to stop! Where women were concerned, Brett Costain was poison.

Trying to be completely honest with herself, Melissa admitted that her attraction to Brett was part of her reluctance to accept the trust fund. And there was something else bothering her too. Did she have the right to deprive Gary's daughter of a relationship with her father's best friend and brother?

Melissa would have no problem doing just that if she were convinced Brett's influence would be a poor one. The problem came from a very real sense that her opinion of him was colored by what had happened between them the night they'd met and his rejection the next day.

The truth was she didn't really know him. The only things she'd heard about him concerned his relationships with women. Other than that subject, Leigh had rarely spoken of Brett at all. To judge him entirely on the merits of his family was unfair. Gary, who was raised by the same parents, had turned out to be a wonderful man. It was altogether possible there was a lot of good in Brett that her sister had assumed Melissa wouldn't want to hear. Leigh certainly hadn't intended to keep Brett from sharing her and Gary's life with the baby.

So what was Melissa to do?

She decided to step back from the problem and avoid him, putting off any decisions until she could look at him with a clear head.

She got down to work after making her decision and managed to catalog and tag every piece of furniture she intended to put in Country and Classics. As she finished scheduling a consultation with the daughter of an old client for early the following week, she glanced at her watch. It was five o'clock and Brett was still hard at work. She had studiously ignored him all day, which wasn't easy with the sound of power tools buzzing in the background.

She fanned herself idly and realized how very hot it had gotten. Guilt crept in. She hadn't even offered Brett as much as a glass of water all day. Ashamed and with Aunt Dora's admonishment always to treat others as you want to be treated echoing in her head, Melissa poured him a glass of sweet tea and carried it to the porch.

Brett stopped pounding the second her shadow fell over him. He looked up and this time he didn't smile. He didn't grin. He just wiped the sweat off his forehead with the back of his hand and nodded a greeting.

"Is that for me?" he asked.

"I was working and I hadn't realized it was so hot out here. Where did you learn to fix a porch?"

Brett walked to a pile of tools and pulled a book from under them. He handed her the thick how-to volume. "There's very little we can't learn from books."

Melissa glanced down at the hardback and thought of all the life lessons she and Leigh had learned from their parents and later Aunt Dora and Uncle Ed. Thinking of their conversation about life and happiness she thought Brett had a lot to learn and she didn't see him learning those lessons from books. But it wasn't her place to tell him so.

Casting about for something to fill the silence, she glanced toward a silver Range Rover he'd parked in the drive. "You traded in your sports car?"

He looked at her as if she'd lost her mind—a mixture of horror and disbelief. "Give up my Beemer? No way. I only rented that for the weekend because I needed to haul the wood."

Melissa couldn't help it. She laughed. Uncle Ed's pickup was still rusting away in the barn over yonder and Izaak still used his father's old wagon to haul wood. Only a Costain and people of their ilk would rent a Range Rover to haul lumber.

"You going to let me in on the joke?" he asked.

Melissa shook her head. It wasn't her job to teach him about the real world even if the hair that fell across his forehead lent him an air of innocence rivaling even the most naive babe in the woods. "I doubt you'd understand," she told him.

"Try me," he dared her, his beard-shadowed chin raised in a challenge. At least this way he didn't looked like a guileless ten-year-old.

What is wrong with your thinking, woman? This is a mover and shaker. A powerful international attorney. He works for heads of multinational, billion-dollar companies. He does not have a slingshot in his back pocket or posies hidden behind his back!

Melissa forced her thoughts to the subject at hand. "How many Beemers and Range Rovers have you seen on these back roads? And how many plain old pickup trucks have you seen?'' she challenged.

''Rovers are sturdy,'' he argued.

The man was completely dense! ''At fifty or sixty thousand dollars a pop, they'd better be.''

He squinted in the glare of the late-afternoon sunlight and looked up at her, scrubbing back his dripping hair. She could almost see him struggling to understand her point. ''Come on. Are you trying to say if I show up with a high-end car when the baby is old enough to understand the difference between a BMW and Chevy it could do some sort of damage to his psyche?''

She sighed. ''No, I'm trying to say you don't have a clue how the other ninety percent live. And it's that attitude that could cause a problem for me later. Do you think Gary would ever have spent his hard-earned money on that kind of luxury?''

Brett glanced at the Rover then back at her and smiled. ''Next time I'll rent a Chevy but I'm not selling my Beemer.''

Melissa nodded, staggered by the smile and a sudden realization. When Brett didn't try to be charming his charm was all the more dangerous. She'd never expected that. The man was positively lethal. All little-boy inquisitive one minute and sexy as all get-out the next.

How was she supposed to talk to him and guard her heart? There had to be some safe subject for them! She looked down at the work he'd done. ''It looks nice. Thank you. I admit every once in a while the boards would moan and I'd begin to wonder if they were going to hold my weight. You got a lot done. I'd like to pay for the wood.''

Brett shook his head and his hair fell across his forehead again. "Consider it a baby gift. I've actually enjoyed the physical work. I don't get a lot of time in the fresh air."

After all his work, Melissa knew she couldn't send him off without at least feeding him. Aunt Dora would haunt her sleep more than Brett already did if she even tried it. In the interest of a good night's rest, she asked, "Would you like to stay for dinner?"

"That'd be great." He smiled and for the second time in less than a minute there was no hidden agenda lurking in his eyes. And for the second time in as many minutes Melissa had to hold on to her heart and soul for dear life.

Before today he'd always been angling for something. A concession. Sex. Something. But when he smiled for real, it lit his pale-gray eyes and told of a greater depth to him than she'd thought possible. Maybe he was more like Gary than she'd thought.

"You're welcome to use the shower," she told him, trying not to attach too much meaning to what she thought she saw. His fixing her porch might still have a hidden agenda. Mightn't it?

"A shower sounds terrific just about now," Brett said. "I have a change of clothes in the Rover. I didn't stop at the motel this morning. I drove straight to the lumberyard when I got down here. I wanted to get an early start since there was so much to do. Sorry I woke you."

Melissa banged around the kitchen minutes later, thinking he hadn't looked the least bit sorry when he'd been ogling her at practically dawn. She threw a slap-dash dinner together and half an hour later Brett joined her in the kitchen. As she finished putting the meal on the table, Melissa ordered her pounding heart to behave. It didn't listen.

"This looks wonderful," he said, sitting where she indicated.

So do you, Melissa thought before taking one last glance at the table. There was leftover roast beef, oven-browned potatoes, a colorful bowl of mixed vegetables and Margaret Abramson's home-baked bread and fresh-churned butter. Most of it was courtesy of his little shopping excursion, but still, she somehow doubted he ever ate this way at the gourmet restaurants he probably frequented.

Deciding she didn't care if he felt the dinner lacked sophistication, she sat across from him and tried not to stare. He was so handsome and self-assured. And he was once again the picture of his aristocratic upbringing in designer clothes and Italian shoes.

So why couldn't her more-than-adequate brain manage to make her unruly heart behave? "I never thanked you for the food you left," she said, knowing nothing separated them so much as the disparity of the classes they belonged to.

"No thanks necessary," he said.

His refusal of her gratitude made him seem superior and arrogant. She hated that he thought he was better than her. If only she hadn't offered him a simple dinner in her simple kitchen.

"Brett, I'm really not as bad off financially as you seem to think. I'd been putting money aside for some time to convert the barn and I have a lot of inventory lined up for the shop already. In fact, it's all around us. I had to put my plans for the shop on hold when Uncle Ed started failing. When he died and Leigh and Gary came down for the funeral, they asked me about the baby. The timing couldn't have been better since I'd pretty much suspended my business so I could take care of Uncle Ed in those final months.''

"That's why he left the farm to you alone, isn't it? Because you gave up everything you'd built for him. I'd wondered about that. Do you ever stop giving? The timing when Leigh and Gary asked you about the baby might have been good, but it must've been a difficult decision. You were going to be giving away your first-born child. They asked too much.''

Melissa felt her cheeks heat. "Leigh would have done the same for me. I know she would. And I'm not pretending it would have been easy to watch them raising her but—''

"Her?'' Brett arched one dark raven's wing of an eyebrow. "Is that a guess? Wishful thinking?''

Still excited over the ultrasound picture that had been done yesterday, Melissa jumped up. She was eager to change the subject and even more anxious to share the first picture of her child, even if it was only a shadowy black-and-white image that a technician had needed to explain.

She handed Brett the picture. "They do these routinely now. And I got lucky. At sixteen weeks they can tell the sex if the baby's in the right position and she was. That's my baby girl.'' Melissa's voice broke and tears she tried to blink back welled up in her eyes.

Leigh had so wanted a little girl.

Not wanting to cry in front of Brett, Melissa quickly excused herself and fled the room. On the way to her grandparents' bath just outside the downstairs bedroom, she caught sight of Leigh staring back at her from the hall mirror and froze in place. The incredible loss of her twin slammed into her once again with a two-ton force.

It was a bittersweet pain that would have taken her to her knees were she not held in place by the sight before her. Leigh but not Leigh. Gone but never farther away than a mirror. Leigh would never age and yet she would. Her own reflection would forever remind Melissa of the incredible bond she and Leigh had shared and the void her loss left.

Melissa didn't know how long she stood there with her fingertips touching the flat cold face on the other side of the glass. She and that other part of her cried silently for both of them. The one lost and the one left behind. Only half of who she was but two people as well.

Was she forever doomed to lose those she loved and relied upon?

Chapter Five

Brett wished Melissa would come back so she could explain what he was supposed to be seeing in the ultrasound print. He stared down at the confusing black-and-white photo trying to see a tiny human form. He felt ignorant and out of touch, sure there was some well-known trick to deciphering the picture.

When several minutes had gone by and Melissa didn't return, he began wondering where she'd gone so suddenly. And why. She'd looked a little upset, he acknowledged. Worried, but feeling like an intruder, Brett cautiously followed and found her in a darkened hall staring at herself in a mirror and crying silent tears. He stepped behind her, very much aware that she didn't realize he was there.

"Melissa? Hey, Melissa," he whispered.

Her eyes shifted a bit and she focused on his reflection. "It's like looking at a pastel version of her, isn't it?'' she asked, tears choking her voice. ''She was so *alive* and *vivid*. How can she be gone?'' Her eyes slid back to her image again. ''And yet never gone. Always staring back at me, taunting me because it isn't her I see.

''She wanted a girl,'' Melissa whispered, her voice as broken as her heart apparently was. Her lower lip quivered and her face started to crumple. ''She wanted that so badly. And now—Oh, God. Leigh!''

To Brett there was nothing scarier in the world than a crying woman, except maybe a crying baby. He had no clue what to do. What was he even doing here? He desperately wanted to run from the intimacy of Melissa's tears and grief. But then he glanced down at the picture he still held.

This scrap of humanity he couldn't even correctly discern had been his brother's fondest wish, as well as Leigh's. Gary had wanted a daughter to cuddle and protect and love just the way he did her mother. And now he would never get to hold her, hear her first cry or later her childish laughter.

''Think of how happy you made the last two weeks of their lives,'' Brett told her, then found himself biting his lip and fighting tears as well.

He hadn't allowed himself to cry for Gary, not even once. He didn't know why for sure. Maybe because there was no one in his life to hold him while he did. Or maybe because he'd been afraid that if he gave in and let himself cry, he'd never stop. Suddenly sharing this crushing grief with the only person in the world who actually shared it and fully understood it was all that mattered to him.

He turned her away from the mirror and into his arms, holding her close. Brett didn't know how long they stood that way just clutching each other and crying silently. But after a while she wrapped her arms around his waist and something shifted in him.

The feel of her in his arms suddenly registered. He felt as if he'd taken a one-hundred-fifty-volt charge to his heart. And he felt like a heel for noticing how perfectly she fitted against him. But, dammit, he wasn't made of stone and had never claimed to be a saint. When he'd had her in his arms that night they'd met, her body had promised ecstasy. She was an unfulfilled promise that he'd never quite gotten out of his system.

Brett swallowed. This was dangerous. She wasn't the kind of woman he got involved with. Ever. And this woman above all others had to stay off-limits.

"Come on," he whispered against her hair. "Let's go sit on that nice safe porch I almost finished for you today." In the shelter of his arms he guided her the few feet down the hall to the dimly lit living room.

Melissa looked up then and the tears in her eyes seemed to be magnifying their clear blue-green color and gave them all the sparkle of precious gems. Her gaze caught his and one of them turned toward the other. He didn't know which one. It didn't seem to matter once their lips met in a charged union he'd always sworn could not have felt the way it had. But once again it did.

Brett cupped her face, his fingers threading in her soft hair, and deepened the kiss. He tasted her tears and probably his. Then Melissa moaned in the back of her throat and Brett broke the kiss, afraid it was a protest—terrified it wasn't.

"We have to stop this. Forget it too. You were right earlier when you pointed out that we come from dif-

ferent worlds.'' He took her hand and put the ultrasound photo into it, but not before the image before
him exploded to life in his mind. Fighting to maintain
his resolve, he continued, ''But our worlds have
crossed into each other's because of her and there's
no way to change that.''

Her expression changed from dreamy to one he'd
have to analyze later. Then she raised her chin and he
knew she meant to challenge him. ''You could just go
back to your world and leave me alone to raise her in
mine.''

He lifted the hand holding the photo and kissed her
fingers, shaking his head. ''I'll be back,'' he said, and
melted back into the deeply shadowed hall.

His whispered promise barely stirred the air.

As he drove north, Brett came to the conclusion that
he'd never get the picture of Melissa's face when he'd
turned away from her out of his head. The hurt and
the fear he'd seen written on her lovely features had
nearly brought him to his knees.

It haunted him for the whole three-and-a-half-hour
drive back to Devon. It berated him the whole time
he unloaded the hand tools he'd bought to rebuild her
porch floor. It tortured him as he stood beneath an
icy-cold shower trying to forget the feel of her in his
arms and her lips under his.

He never should have given in to his desire for her
again, but then he'd exacerbated the mistake by dis-
counting the importance of the kiss. Now what?

She didn't deserve to have him in her life, but the
bottom line was he couldn't change that. Because a
new truth had been slowly dawning on him all day.
From the moment the baby had been conceived, Gary

had expected Brett to be more than a mere uncle to his little niece. Gary had made him more when he'd asked him to be the baby's godfather. Which meant his obligation went beyond a trust fund, beyond birthday and Christmas gifts and appearing every once in a while with pats on the head and infrequent applause for a job well done. His obligation went beyond what it normally would have because of Gary's death. And it continued to grow even as the child grew in Melissa's body.

When he'd looked at the ultrasound as he'd put it in her hand, something magical had happened. He'd somehow seen the baby's little face emerge from the specks and dots that made up the ultrasound photo. He supposed it might be a fanciful notion but at that moment, on the heels of remembering all of his brother's hopes and desires for his child, had come the realization of everything his brother would miss. And Brett had suddenly known he had to do even more than he'd thought he would ever have to do.

He had to find a way to actually fill in for Gary. To experience as much of that little girl's life as Melissa would allow. For Gary's sake. For the baby's. And, God help him, for his own sake as well.

Which still left him trying to find a way to convince Melissa he wasn't the ogre she thought, even though his actions in the past and even tonight said he was. He had to convince Melissa he was one of the good guys.

And he would. Even if he had to camp on her doorstep to do it. Brett, by now back to unloading the rented SUV, stopped in his tracks, set the big crosscut/miter saw down on the back seat and stared at his reflection in the glass as a plan coalesced in his mind.

That's exactly what he'd do. He'd camp on her doorstep.

Or close to it. Right across the street from the entrance of her drive there was a little box of a house secluded within a tall copse of trees. And it was for sale. The bungalow wasn't his style, and wasn't in the greatest shape, but he could easily hire a contractor to make it bearable. Eventually he could sell it to one of the developers his detective had mentioned were beginning to buy up land in the area. It would be a good investment all around.

He had a bundle of vacation time stored up. Even his father, one of the senior partners of Brett's firm and a workaholic of the first water, had mentioned that Brett was due some time off. So he'd take a leave of absence. Go on a sabbatical! What better cause was there than winning a chance with Melissa? Well, not with Melissa per se but a chance to win her approval.

Melissa slowed her car as she approached the base of her drive but rather than turn in she stopped and looked toward a flash of bright color off to the left. If she wasn't mistaken, there in the drive of the old Jacobs place sat a bright yellow pickup truck.

Until a few weeks ago, the Arts-and-Crafts-era bungalow and its remaining five-acre tract of prime farmland had been up for sale. When Melissa had seen the sale sign go up she'd worried a developer would buy it. She had no problem with progress and quite frankly the more people who moved into the area the better chance she had for her design business and Country and Classics to succeed. But somehow, seeing the old place torn down would have been sad. Then the Sold sign had appeared and she'd learned through the grapevine that it had gone to a private buyer who had plans to move in and renovate the little bungalow.

Grateful to the nameless, faceless owners of the cheery yellow pickup she decided to pay a call on her new neighbor with one of the pies she'd baked that morning. Ten minutes later, Melissa started down her drive carrying Aunt Dora's favorite basket. Inside she'd nestled a blueberry pie and a set of Margaret's lovely place mats as a welcome gift. She'd also changed out of the suit she'd worn for a consultation with a new client on Flora Corner Road.

As she strolled down her drive, she was glad she'd walked, even though the sun was hot and the breeze seemed to have died. The day was bright with promise, just like her future. The commission she'd secured to decorate the six-bedroom, seven-bath house her new clients had just bought would be a lucrative job all on its own. But the word-of-mouth business she'd get when Mrs. Edgar started meeting her neighbors would help fill her calendar for months to come.

Unfortunately, by the time she'd crossed the road and begun to pick her way up the blue stone-and-weed-infested drive, she'd begun to rethink the walk. The heat had become oppressive and a thin sheen of perspiration coated her skin. She hoped her new neighbor would ask her in to sit and offer her a cool drink, otherwise the walk back could be really uncomfortable.

Pasting on a smile she no longer felt quite as enthusiastically as she had, Melissa knocked on the screen door. When the inner door opened, she couldn't see the face of the person who came to answer her knock through the dark, aged screening. She knew by

the height and width of the shoulders that it was
a man.

"Hi, there," she said as he started to swing open
the old aluminum screen door. "I just dropped by to
welcome you to the neighborhood. I own the place
across the road. I baked a blue...ber...ry..." Melissa
trailed off and could only stare. Then the world tilted.

"Melissa!"

As if from far away, Melissa heard the utter panic
in Brett's voice. The basket was slipping from her
fingers.

In fascinated horror, Melissa watched as Brett
grabbed the falling basket with one hand and wrapped
his other arm around her. Only then did she realize
the basket hadn't been the only thing in danger of
crashing to the ground in a heap. The tilting world
went weightless in the next second as Brett smoothly
transferred the basket to the hand at her waist and
swung her into his arms.

"I thought it was only mad dogs and Englishmen
who went out in the heat of the day," he muttered as
he entered the cool house with her still in his arms.

She frowned, trying to figure out why he had any
right to sound so upset. She was the one who'd sus-
tained a shock, after all. She blinked, furiously trying
to clear her vision as well as her thoughts.

"What do you think you're doing?" she demanded
as he carried her deep into the house.

"A quick analysis would tell a careful observer I'm
keeping you and whatever you have in this basket
from doing a nosedive on my front step."

"That isn't what I mean and you know it. And put
me down! I'm perfectly fine now."

"You don't look fine to me," he growled as he set

her in one of two straight-back chairs that flanked the old brick fireplace and placed the basket on the floor. Then he rushed away to the kitchen, returning with a cool glass of water within seconds.

Melissa took the glass and, while taking a few short sips, looked around hoping to orient herself. The room snared her attention in a split second with its incongruous combination of shabby and chic. Faded cabbage-rose wallpaper fought with a modern steel-blue leather sectional sofa and industrial-style glass-top tables. Her fascination had nothing to do with current decorating trends, however. It was the idea of Brett living in so inelegant and cobbled-together a room. She found it almost laughable.

What wasn't at all amusing was the lack of warning she'd had that he'd taken up residence so near her own home. Even his BMW parked in the drive would have hinted at the shock ahead.

"What is that in your driveway?" she demanded, then could have screamed when he grinned.

"It's a Chevy pickup. It's even five years old. It has eighty thousand miles on it. I thought you'd understand."

It took her a second or two to connect the late-model pickup with her criticism of his choice of rental cars. His smirk irritated her. So he was a fast learner. All that said was that his choice was insincere. That he was trying to sway her with his adaptability. But he was still out to impress—still after something.

With her escalating annoyance making her feel stronger, Melissa stood. "What I understand is that it was an effort and not a natural choice. And what I'd appreciate is an explanation of what you think you're doing here. Better yet, I'd appreciate you disappearing in a puff of smoke.''

His gray eyes turned steely pewter. ''I refuse to be ashamed of my tax bracket. I've earned every damned dime I have through hard work and careful investing. All my parents gave me was food, clothing and an education. Maybe my father's name gave me an in with his firm but I earned my partnership.''

''I never said you should be ashamed.''

She really hadn't meant to discount or minimize his success or his hard work. He'd just never understand why the switch to the pickup annoyed her more than his usual choice of the high-end cars he could easily afford. It had been a waste of time even to get into it with him. ''I'll make my question more specific. What are you doing here in this house?''

''I bought the property.'' He bent and picked up the basket he'd placed on the floor minutes before and dipped his head toward it. ''I thought you'd come across the road to welcome your new neighbor but you don't seem happy to see me.''

Melissa snatched the basket from him. ''Quit the smart-aleck stuff, Brett. You knew I wouldn't be happy about this.''

Brett's expression lost its taunting quality. ''No, I didn't think you'd be happy about it, but I was trying to keep it light because this doesn't have to be a big deal. Would you just sit down and listen to what I have to say? You still look a little pale.''

Knowing a nosedive, as he'd called it, wouldn't be good for the baby, and since he seemed genuinely worried about her, Melissa nodded and sank into the chair. Brett smiled sadly and took the basket from her lap, setting it on the floor between them.

"I know finding me living across the road from you had to come as a big shock and I'm sorry," he said as he settled on the edge of the leather sectional. "I didn't want to argue with you and you have to admit telling you ahead of time would have led to a disagreement. I don't want to upset you. I know it isn't good for either you or the baby, but I didn't have a choice. I have a proposal for you. If I can't stick it out living here until the baby is born, I'll disappear from both your lives without a peep."

"Brett, I can't stop you from living here, but I don't have to like it. I can see what I get out of putting up with you living across the road till you cave in and cry uncle—no pun intended. But where's the advantage for you and where's my *dis*advantage in this."

"I want you to agree to let me be a part of your life until my niece is born and I want your promise to accept the trust fund if I last that long. After she's born you'll have control over how much I see of her."

"What do you mean 'be a part of my life'?"

"I want the opportunity I asked for once before. You don't trust me. You don't forgive me for what I said the first day I came here about suing for custody. I want to be allowed to try to change your mind. I'd like you to learn to like me too, but I'll settle for tolerance."

There still had to be a *but* in there somewhere. "And if I don't agree?"

He shrugged. "Melissa, this isn't a threat. If you don't agree and you get into any kind of a jam, I'll have to assume you'll care more about the baby than your mistrust of me or your pride. Because I'll be waiting right here to help you any way I can. There's a gamble involved in this for me too. You might not give me a chance. Or I might not be able to stick it out till she's born. Even if I do, you might find you still can't trust me to see her and be a part of her life. Hell, I took a big chance buying this place and coming here again. You could sic your sheriff friend on me.''

Melissa nodded. He *had* taken a big gamble. And he was essentially leaving her in the driver's seat. Still the future was a big worry for her. She would be a mother to this child for the rest of her life. And Brett would be her uncle. ''Suppose the upshot of your wager is a yes all around?''

Brett pursed his lips, the look in his eyes unfathomable. ''I'll keep this place and visit—alone—whenever we both agree I can. That way she won't be exposed to the life I lead away from here. Fair enough?''

It did sound fair. More than fair. Especially since there was no way jet-setting Brett Costain, Esquire, would last a month in this tiny bungalow. What did she have to lose?

Your heart, a small voice inside her warned and she acknowledged there was a chance he could hurt her again if she let him get too close. He had a strange sort of power over her she couldn't seem to fight, even with all she knew about him. But what choice did she have? He was Gary's brother. She had to give him a chance to prove himself even though she was nearly sure he'd fail.

But what if he doesn't? the voice asked. He had just made what amounted to a lifetime commitment to her daughter. He would be around a long time with his sexy grins, and even sexier body.

''All right. But I have one steadfast rule. What happened before you left the last time you were here can never happen again. Understood?''

"I agree wholeheartedly. I believe I said much the same thing before I left. But denying what we feel for each other isn't the answer to the problem. We're attracted to each other. Hell, together we're explosive. We have to acknowledge it and the disaster giving in would cause in order to deal with it. I mean you can hardly stand the sight of me and you aren't exactly the type of woman I gravitate toward."

Uncomfortable, Melissa stood. "Fine. I'm not going to deny what your mirror tells you every morning, but there's one factor you seem to forget. I still find you appallingly shallow and amoral. That alone is deterrent enough for me."

Brett's eyes flared, but he stayed seated, maintaining his relaxed posture. Then he recovered and shot her that damned lady-killer grin of his. "But what will you do after I prove you wrong?"

Melissa headed for the door but stopped and turned, unable to let his challenge go unanswered. "It's a chance in a million, Brett. Forewarned is forearmed. And Leigh did a good job all these years of letting me know how lucky I was you showed your true colors as quickly as you did. I imagine I'll see you around."

"You'll see me for another few minutes," he growled, following her to the door and outside. "You are not walking back home after the walk over nearly knocked you flat. I'll drive you home."

Grateful, she headed for the passenger side of the bright pickup but she couldn't let him have the last word. "Fine but it was you and your sudden appearance that nearly knocked me flat."

He grinned as he climbed behind the wheel. "Why, Ms. Abell, I do believe that's the nicest thing you've ever said to me."

Chapter Six

Brett tucked a napkin under the fork then laid his hand on the teapot to check that it was still nice and warm. After another quick survey of the scene he'd set on the porch to make sure it was perfect, he knocked on Melissa's door.

"Brett?" she said, her voice wary and full of questions. He hated that tone in her voice. Why did she persist in seeing him as a fiend come to destroy her life?

Because you showed up here and threatened to do just that, you jackass!

He pushed off that depressing thought. He'd pour on the charm. Become indispensable. He'd make her like him. Then she'd want her little girl to have him for an uncle. Satisfied his plan was still on track, he reached to open her tattered wooden screen door. She was dressed in a pale-blue, tailored suit. But even decked out for some sort of business meeting, she looked soft and sweet. Infinitely eatable.

"I brought breakfast," he said, quickly banishing his unruly thoughts. If he didn't get a handle on his lust for this woman—*the mother of his niece*—he'd ruin everything or drive himself insane inside of a week. Maybe both. What was it about her that always sent his mind on a sexual tangent?

"Why would you bring me breakfast?" she asked, clearly confused.

"You said you were trying to get your business started again. I imagine that's a lot to handle. I wanted to make sure you started your day right. And it looks as if I wasn't wrong to worry." He gestured toward the power bar in her hand. "That isn't as healthy as it looks. Have you ever read the nutritional information on those things?"

She looked at the chocolate-flavored bar in her hand. "It's supposed to have a lot of vitamins and it's fast." She checked her watch. "I have a meeting at ten."

Brett plucked the offending bar from her unresisting fingers. "Good thing I got up early." He gestured to the card table he'd set up on her porch. A variety of fresh fruit sat in a bowl in the center of the old table. He'd filled a soup tureen with the scrambled eggs and had even liberally sprinkled crumbled bacon on them the way his housekeeper did. Thank God the bungalow's previous owner had left that ancient cookbook in the kitchen cupboard and that bacon came with directions on the package.

"This looks lovely," she said, walking warily to the table and taking a seat. "I didn't know you could cook."

Mindful of her reaction to the pickup, he thought he'd better opt for the truth up front. After all, it wasn't as if breakfast hadn't turned out just fine. He sat down across from her prepared to be honest. "I can't. At least I couldn't until I found an old cookbook in my new kitchen. Mrs. Jacobs left a couple other books you should have a look at for your new shop. One is a real hoot. It's from the twenties or thirties on how to be a proper housewife."

She was still staring at him in disbelief. "You needed a recipe for scrambled eggs?"

Leave it to Melissa to zero in on his deficiencies. He picked up the power bar and nodded toward it. "I usually just grab something quick too, but the eggs are safe. I told you I can learn anything from a book."

She chuckled and dug into the eggs, dishing a liberal amount onto a plate. She passed it into his hands and slid his plate from in front of him, serving herself a much smaller portion.

Brett groped for his fork. "Here, take some of these back. That's not enough to keep a gnat alive."

She shook her head. "I'm not a gnat. And this is fine."

"But the book said pregnant women should have three balanced meals a day and even snacks to get all the nutrients they need."

"One egg and one piece of toast *is* a balanced meal."

"Then at least make sure you drink your orange juice and have another piece of toast. This is supposed to be a meal not a snack."

"What book are you talking about? Surely you aren't listening to an old cookbook on the subject of eating during pregnancy."

He chuckled. "No. I picked up a few books on pregnancy back in Philadelphia. I haven't had a lot of time to read them since these last two and a half weeks at the office have been so hectic. I did get as far as nutrition and how important it is, though. The rest looks fascinating."

Melissa stared at him, a slight frown creasing her smooth forehead. "I never thought about the law firm. How are you going to live here? It's so far from Philadelphia. What about your career?"

"I'm a full partner so I get a lot of perks. I cleared my calendar, talked to my clients and took a leave of absence."

"Just like that? But Brett, isn't that a huge financial hit?"

It hadn't been a snap at all, and one of the three senior partners had been more than curious about his reasons. He'd done quite a bit of prevaricating, not wanting anyone to get wind of the baby sooner than necessary. Luckily his father, the second of the three senior partners, was still handling a court action in Spain. The third, a man well past retirement age, had just smiled and wished Brett well.

But Brett didn't go into all that with Melissa. Instead he told her, "I can afford the time. Don't worry. I have a healthy portfolio and plenty of ready cash to keep the wolf from the door. Nothing is more important to me than being here for you and Gary's child right now. I'm usually too busy to spend even a fifth of my income anyway since I don't have any housing expenses. Until now, that is."

Brett smiled and his mind drifted across the road to the little house he'd moved into just yesterday. He actually saw possibilities in the bungalow as a little retreat away from the pressure of his normal life. He felt more relaxed here than he had in years. Maybe this sojourn wouldn't be as treacherously boring as he'd first feared.

He'd talked a good story with Melissa yesterday, trying to sound sure he could handle living on a one-time tobacco farm in a tiny box of a house. But he'd been anything but sure. Before she'd arrived, he'd been pacing and looking around himself at the faded, stained wallpaper, at how badly the furniture he'd rented fit in and wondering what he was trying to prove. Then Melissa had come to his door, welcome basket in hand and his heart had rolled over in his chest. For one glorious moment he'd thought she was actually there to welcome *him*—not some faceless neighbor.

Earning one of those freewheeling smiles from her had suddenly become more important to him than taking his next breath. Only because it would mean she finally trusted him, he quickly told himself. That was all he wanted—or could want—from the mother of Gary's baby. He'd rejected her once when she'd offered more and he'd learned a painful lesson. He would never be good for a woman like her.

"I guess your parents will miss you while you're gone," Brett heard Melissa say, and he stiffened before he could stop himself. "At least, I assume they will. You *are* closer to your parents than Gary was, aren't you? I mean, you live in the carriage house you offered me at Bellfield. Right?"

He nearly groaned. She'd seen his reaction. It was always hard to talk about his relationship with his parents. Harder still with Gary, who was the only one who had understood, gone. But then again Brett didn't want to be guilty by association later if his mother caused trouble over the baby. He guessed he could explain a little. Just enough so that she knew what kind of relationship he had with them, and that, in essence, it was no better than Gary's had been.

"I live at Bellfield because it's convenient and expedient," he lied only a little. It was convenient and expedient for his parents. He traveled a lot but not as much as they did. Someone had to make sure regular maintenance got done on the estate and with him handling it, his parents were forced to keep in touch.

"You mean you aren't close to them either?"

"Not many people are close to my parents, least of all either of their children."

"Oh. That's...so sad." She looked down at her empty plate then back up at him. He could see pity in her startlingly blue-green eyes and was sorry he'd said as much as he had. What kind of protector would she see him as if she knew he'd always wanted more of a relationship from the people who would threaten her child's happiness.

"I'd better get going," she said into the resulting silence. "This was a lovely surprise and a nice way to start the day. Thank you, Brett."

Melissa hurried inside, then she was back with her purse and keys in her hand and a huge binder tucked under her arm. "Well, I'm off. Thanks again." She started down the steps but turned back. "You intended to come back to Maryland, didn't you?"

"I think so. Yeah," he answered.

She sighed and shook her head. "I can't figure you out. For the record, if you're trying to throw me off balance, you're succeeding."

Brett watched her get into her car and tool down

the drive. She wasn't the only one thrown off balance. He'd turned his whole world upside down, and he was very much afraid he hadn't done it for the baby or even Melissa, but because of the way he felt when Melissa was near. And that meant he was in big trouble.

The problem was bigger still because so far he was loving every minute of it.

Shaking his head, Brett piled the dishes back in the box he'd transported them in, took the bowl of fruit inside to put on her kitchen counter, then got down to planning the day.

Melissa was grateful for Brett's surprise breakfast two hours later when her client was still vacillating between marble or slate in her foyer and kitchen. Why did people hire designers then not utilize the skills they were paying them for?

What was worse, since Heady Barker had practically excluded her from the discussion with the builder, Melissa's mind kept slipping back to breakfast and the look in Brett's eyes when he'd all but confessed to being nearly a stranger to his own parents.

She thought of Bellfield and tried to picture Gary and Brett spending their early childhoods there. And couldn't. Except for that darned pool house, every nook and cranny she'd seen of the estate was stiffly formal. Unfortunately, she could picture Brett in the pool house only too well.

Except he wasn't a child at play. He was a heavily breathing, aroused lover, hovering over her during her first hot and heavy petting session. And he was looking at her with need and wonder mixed with confusion in his eyes, and all because she'd asked him if making love was always so overpoweringly miraculous. Back then, that same sadness she'd seen earlier had invaded those silvery eyes of his, and he'd rested his forehead on hers.

"No," he'd said. "It's not, sweetheart, and miracles just don't happen in my life. I think it's time we got back before we're missed."

For the first time, maybe because Brett had apologized for what had followed, Melissa saw past the two of them on that chaise to the setting around them. It had been like being transported to another world. A sensual experience all on its own. A trip into the Italian countryside. A villa in the hills surrounding the Mediterranean could not have been more romantic. Elegant and informal at the same time. No wonder she had succumbed so easily.

"What do you think, Melissa? I guess I should let you earn your fee," Heady Barker said.

In a flash Melissa was back in the present but with a vision of that villa setting still clinging to her consciousness. And that vision was about to save her bacon. Or earn it! She had the answer. At least a professional one. She had a feeling a personal answer had been somewhere in that crystal-clear memory as well but she didn't have time to search for it.

"Heady, from what I see, we need to come up with a compromise. Your vision is a casual décor, especially in the kitchen and keeping room, but you basically have a blank slate to create on. You're the easiest to please. However, your husband wants formal public rooms with his recent Italian purchases being utilized. And unfortunately, Mr. De Antonio's homes are strictly American Colonial designs. I think the solution is staring us in the face. If we start with the marble in the foyer," she began as she dug through the builder's many samples, selecting just the right colors and textures to fulfill the theme she'd visualized for the Barker's million-dollar home. What emerged was a wonderful blending of rich tile and faux painting. A little tweaking to the exterior of the house and all was settled.

On the drive home she realized she was simply exhausted. She got tired so easily these days it was ridiculous. And aggravating clients, or more correctly their demanding husbands, just tired her more. Goodness, she'd started daydreaming in the middle of a consultation, and about an incident she should have put behind her years ago.

It was only luck her mental tangent had not only gained her the thanks of her client but the gratitude of the builder who promised to recommend her to other buyers. Unfortunately, it had also given her something disturbing to consider about the past.

Brett had figured out she was a virgin that night and rather than proceed with an easy conquest, he'd been the one to back off, and she was almost sure he'd done it for her sake. Didn't that mean he wasn't as much like his father as everyone said? And he'd stopped without a word of derision or complaint over her naiveté. She wasn't so inexperienced that she hadn't seen or heard of a few mild temper tantrums in physically charged situations like that. Didn't that say something positive about Brett as a person?

When Melissa reached home a little while later, she was surprised to find Brett hard at work on the porch once again. She didn't know why she hadn't expected that, but she hadn't. Now that he was practically in residence, she'd thought he'd keep his efforts at more personal contacts like that morning's breakfast and not tackle such an uncomfortable and physical job as the porch. Especially since it didn't put them in close proximity.

Apparently she'd been wrong.

He ambled over to her car and opened the door for her. "Hi. I'll stop for a while so you can nap," he said.

She mentally blinked. She hadn't taken a nap since she was five years old. Did she look that bad? "Why would I need to nap?"

"The book said pregnant women often get tired and should nap rather than risk exhaustion. You don't want to deplete your immune system."

Melissa found she had enough energy to raise an inquiring eyebrow. "I thought you didn't have much time to read," she asked, a little embarrassed that she herself had read little of the pregnancy book she'd bought. She carefully followed her doctor's advice but every time she started to read up on the months to come—especially labor and delivery—complete and utter panic set in.

"I had plenty of time last night to read," Brett was saying. "Did you know your blood volume doubles or close to it? It's no wonder women get tired and have to eat more. By the way, did you have lunch yet?"

She sighed. Apparently it was time she stopped pretending to be an ostrich. "No, I didn't know about the blood volume thing and I haven't eaten."

He looked at her a little strangely and said, "Okay, then. You go get into something comfortable while I get cleaned up. We'll scare something up for you to eat while you tell me what about this meeting was so much harder than the one you had yesterday.''

Melissa sat in her car watching Brett walk back across the yard, dusting sawdust off himself as he went. ''Who are you and what did you do with the real Brett Costain?'' she muttered, then gathered her things to go fix lunch with the alien life form masquerading as Brett Costain, noted international attorney and reputed womanizing creep.

How had her nice, safe, insulated world been turned upside down by the presence of one person—alien life form or not?

Chapter Seven

Melissa woke from her enforced nap to the sound of her ringing telephone. Feeling muzzy-headed and not quite with it, she reached for the phone on her nightstand. "'Lo," she all but grumbled.

"Uh-oh. Somebody still sounds wiped out. I'll call back later."

Hearing Brett's voice sent Melissa's pulse skittering all over the place. She was awake all right, and this reaction to him had to stop! She couldn't make him leave, but she couldn't let him make her want him either. And she positively couldn't get used to hearing his voice or relying on his continued presence should she need him. Even if he stayed till the baby was born, he'd be gone soon afterward.

"I am not wiped out," she told him through gritted teeth. She had to find a way to keep him at a distance.

"I never was. You interrupted me. I was...I was... thinking."

"Whatever you say," he said, his tone tinged with disbelief. "I decided to cook dinner," he continued. "Interested in taking a chance on a novice chef? I even have this wonderful blueberry pie some nice neighbor lady gave me yesterday to welcome me to the neighborhood."

"Someday you're going to die of terminal smart mouth, Brett Costain."

He chuckled. "I'm not sure that's possible."

She ignored the dance something did along her spine and refused to attribute it to his sexy chuckle. "It is if your blueberry-pie-baking neighbor takes her uncle's shotgun to you."

"Has anyone ever told you you're grumpy when you first wake up?"

Leigh had. Her parents and aunt and uncle had. It would be no different with Brett. Soon he'd be gone too, and, unlike her family, he'd be gone by his own choice. And she'd be alone. Alone to face childhood disease and injury. Bills and teacher's notes. Alone. Why did she always end up alone?

"No one's ever around when I wake up, Brett, unlike some people I could mention who have a revolving door on their bedroom."

"My, but sister Leigh spent a lot of time enhancing my rep, didn't she? Believe me, except for Gary no one's ever been around when I've woken up either. That's a little too domestic a scene for me."

Melissa had no comment to make on that. She wasn't even sure how she felt about it or about having him toss off the information as easily as if it were his favorite color or food. Though it was entirely inappropriate, pity led the laundry list of her feelings ahead of anger and disgust. Was he afraid to let someone get close?

She ruthlessly squelched her kinder impulses where he was concerned. "T.M.I., Brett," she said instead.

"T.M.I.? Wasn't that the nuclear power plant that almost melted down in the late seventies?"

"It means you just gave me too much information. I don't particularly want to hear about your love life or, more specifically, your sex life."

"There's a difference?" he asked, a grin in his voice.

"My point exactly. I doubt you've ever loved anyone not staring back at you from your bathroom mirror."

There was a telling moment of silence then. "I loved Gary or I probably wouldn't be here." He sighed. "Are you coming to dinner or not?"

"Not," she said, then hit the disconnect button. Unfortunately, she was immediately sorry—for what she'd said and for hanging up. His grief had been thick in his voice when he'd mentioned Gary. And there'd been a wealth of loneliness there too. One of the reasons she'd moved out of Gary and Leigh's house on the day of the funeral to return so quickly to St. Marys County was that she had people here at home who shared her grief over Leigh. There were Izaak and Margaret. Hunter Long. Other friends from high school who knew both her and Leigh. Even old Mrs. Jacobs had cried with her when Melissa visited her elderly former neighbor at St. Marys Nursing Home.

Melissa thought of the mourners at Leigh and Gary's funeral. The Costain family, dry-eyed to a person, had expressed their shock and condolences, but it had been clear none of them really grieved the loss of their relative and his wife. The only tears shed were hers and those of Gary and Leigh's friends and co-workers. Gary's parents, after arriving late, hadn't even approached the caskets after the service concluded. Their lateness had even robbed Brett of being where he'd clearly longed to be, at his brother's side that final time.

And then she remembered Brett's tears seeping into her hair as they'd stood in her darkened hall grieving over their mutual loss. It occurred to her that Brett might be searching for something more in his move to St. Marys County than just winning a place in her baby girl's life. She didn't have a clue what he was seeking but, then again, she suspected Brett wasn't even aware how over the top his move to the wilds of southern Maryland really was.

She found herself wanting to help him and she knew she should try. He was, after all, her child's only uncle and he wanted to be active in their lives. In just one day she'd come to see that he was stubborn enough to stick it out till the baby was born. Which meant she'd soon have a decision to make concerning three lives. Hers, her baby's and Brett's.

Melissa knew deep in her heart that though it would be easier to dismiss him from their lives, it wouldn't necessarily be fair. It was true that he would leave, but he'd said he wanted to visit. If she did let him visit from time to time, they would need to deal with each other for years to come. And she couldn't do that while harboring all this resentment and conflicting feelings.

Was she too small a person not to finally and truly forgive him his slip in judgment when she'd suffered the same slip? She had been just as much an adult, and therefore just as much at fault in their pool-house interlude as Brett, and it was time she acknowledged it. She had to face reality. Sex didn't mean commitment to a majority of people the way it did to her. Brett wasn't alone in his outlook or lifestyle.

Before she could change her mind, Melissa punched Redial so she could apologize for her moodiness and accept Brett's invitation.

An hour later Brett watched utter disbelief paint itself across Melissa's features as she stared at him across his kitchen table. She blinked then glanced down at the plate he'd set before her. "I hope you don't expect me to eat all of this."

"It's exactly what's left of a balanced diet for today taking into consideration what you ate for breakfast and lunch." He jumped up and went to get the hardbound book he'd bought on pregnancy. "It says here that every day you're supposed to have a quart of milk or its equivalent in cheese, yogurt, even ice cream. The grilled-cheese sandwich handled some of that. Two eggs and you only had about one for breakfast. Two servings of protein foods and the bacon this morning is the only one you've had of those. You've had neither of the two servings of green vegetables it recommends."

She sighed. "Still. There are a lot of vegetables Brett."

He pointed to the page on vegetables. "Look, it says a quarter to a half cup is a serving. I made the spinach to go with the corn. You have to have five servings of yellow or orange vegetables each week. Technically, you need another serving of vegetables today. And the baked potato is one of three you need for the week.''

Melissa rolled her eyes. ''Gee, are you sure you didn't leave anything out?''

He frowned and checked the book. ''Not by my calculation.'' He ran through the list quickly. ''No, I don't think I missed a thing.''

''You're not kidding with this, are you?'' She gazed at him with a mixture of surprise and warmth in her pretty blue-green eyes.

Brett tried to ignore the wild surge of desire her tender regard made him feel. *Warm* was way too mild a word. *Hot.* Really *hot* was closer to it. But it was a moot point. He was leaving after the baby was born, and Melissa wasn't the kind of woman a man left behind.

''No. I'm not kidding. Until I read all this last night I didn't understand how completely you're connected to the baby. You really are eating for two.''

''My pamphlet on diet from my doctor doesn't say any of that. It just says eat a balanced diet. If I eat the way that book of yours says I should, I won't fit in the front door of my house. No, I'll be as big as my house.''

Brett cocked his head and looked at her. How could she be worried about how she looked? She was perfect. ''You don't even look pregnant.'' If Gary hadn't told him, and she hadn't confirmed it any number of times, he'd never guess she was pregnant at all. Although the book said women often didn't ''show'' in their first pregnancy until the fifth and sometimes even their sixth month, it worried him. Suppose all the upset she'd had thus far had damaged the baby somehow?

"Believe me, not a pair of pants in my closet are comfortable anymore. That suit I wore today has the only skirt that'll button, and that was uncomfortable." She shrugged. "Other than that I can't say I feel very different—except I tire more easily and loose dresses are all I want to wear. The doctor says I'm very lucky. I do cry for almost no reason sometimes, but since it's usually about Leigh and Gary, I don't know if it's the baby or grief."

"You have to keep your spirits up. Last night I read that the baby can feel your emotional state. I shouldn't have kept appearing out of the blue. It upset you. I didn't realize..." Brett paused.

"It was a shock to find you opening that door," she said, reinforcing his decision.

He'd never taken chances like these—moving to St. Marys County or the chance he was about to take. He'd known since early in the afternoon after leaving her to nap what he had to do. He just hadn't expected it to be this hard. "I'm sorry. I knew upset wasn't good but I never realized how bad it could be for the baby. If having me here is too much for you, I'll leave." The words inexplicably nearly stuck in his throat. "But I won't leave the country. You'll be able to reach me any time. Leaving wouldn't be what I want. I think you need someone close by in case you need help. But I can't let what I think is my duty to Gary and his baby adversely affect you."

Brett found himself holding his breath and silently begging for the chance to help. To stay. Hard on his pride though it would be, he would gladly beg for that chance but he didn't want to pressure her in any way. He was very afraid he'd already pressured her too much. This shouldn't mean this much but he knew it did. Then she shook her head and he released the pent-up breath in his lungs.

"I was shocked to find you on my doorstep and upset by the things you said that first day. And I don't wholly trust you. But I've had a change of heart just as you have. You're Annalise's uncle."

"Annalise?"

"It's the name they'd picked for a girl. Lise was our mother's name and apparently someone named Annie was important to Gary."

Brett smiled wistfully. "That was the name of our last nanny." She'd been important to him as well.

Melissa chuckled. "You had a nanny named Annie. Nanny Annie?"

Brett nodded and felt the smile grow as the memory blossomed in his mind. Nanny Annie was exactly what he and Gary had called her. She'd been a constant in their lives. A kindly young woman with plain brown hair who'd always smelled like flowers. His smile faded as another memory surfaced.

"My mother dismissed Annie because my father turned his roving eye in her direction. Mother said it was for Annie's own good."

He didn't want Melissa's pity, so he didn't add that he'd been practically snatched from Annie's arms and packed off to Aldon, an exclusive boys' school in upstate New York to keep it from happening again with another nanny. He and Gary had spent the rest of their childhood in that cold boys' school and at summer camps and relatives' homes for holidays.

"That was so unfair," Melissa said.

Brett shrugged. "Leigh once told me one of your uncle's favorite sayings was 'Fair is a weather forecast.'"

Melissa smiled wistfully. "Uncle Ed was quite the armchair philosopher all right."

"Who just happened to be right in this case. Don't feel so sorry for the poor little rich boy. Your life wasn't too terrific either."

"But my parents didn't shunt us aside the way Gary said your parents did. My mom and dad were killed in an accident. And we went to a home where we were loved. We all survive some degree of difficulty getting to our adult years but it has to hurt more when the pain is avoidable, deliberate and inflicted by parents."

She had the truth of that. "When I was little, Gary used to tell me stories about the better, happier life we'd have when we grew up. I'd fall asleep dreaming of the world he described. I came here so your Annalise would never feel anything but happy and secure. Maybe that isn't possible, but I'd sure like to try making that dream of Gary's come true for his child. I just want to help."

Melissa nodded. "Then help." She grinned. "To tell you the truth, this whole pregnancy and childbirth process is getting a little overwhelming the closer it gets. Just don't make me fat."

Brett couldn't believe how heartened he was by her simple acceptance of his aid. It had been nearly unconditional. Of course, her one condition hadn't been his goal in spite of what she thought. She was going to round out according to his literature, but he wanted her to do it healthfully. He only hoped seeing her obviously pregnant would help drown the fire of his desire for her—or it was going to be a long, long string of months.

Melissa left soon after dinner and Brett sat up far into the night, reading and reflecting on the evening with Melissa. Beyond being a good person, she was funny and charming and would make an excellent mother. The fact that she was a desirable woman was a current complication, but he was sure that as time moved forward—with her stomach following suit—he would feel less and less attraction toward her.

His plan as to how he'd deal with her on a daily basis without getting too up close and personal was simple. He'd survey her life and handle the things that needed doing but not intrude on her privacy or let her come to mean too much to him. He'd be leaving by Thanksgiving.

He fell asleep on his sofa making mental lists of all the things that needed doing just on the house alone, while trying not to think of doing the one thing he couldn't do. And that was feeling her soft sweet lips under his again.

Chapter Eight

"Would it bother you if I did a little straightening up around here?" Brett asked from the doorway of her office off the living room.

Melissa looked up from her computer screen. Honestly, she hadn't gotten just an uncle for her child. In the last two days, Brett Costain, international attorney, had somehow transformed himself into Dr. Spock, Mr. Fix-it, Mr. Clean and a very male version of good old Martha Harris—old-time cookbook author and food-fiend. So far though, he'd at least limited his scope to the kitchen.

And driving her insane!

"Straightening up? What needs straightening?" she asked.

He shrugged. "I really meant cleaning. I noticed the place is a little...uh...dusty."

Melissa checked her watch and saw it was only ten

in the morning. She should have known breakfast dishes would keep him out of her hair for only so long now that he'd finished the porch floor. Having a bored workaholic around the house was tiring—just watching him. And that was without mentioning the memories just watching him move around the house resurrected to haunt her sleep.

Unfortunately, she couldn't argue his observation on the condition of the house. Between her pregnancy, getting the design business up and running and planning Country and Classics, she just didn't have the energy for housework. And the place had gone to pot even before this. During Uncle Ed's illness, it had been all she could do to just care for him and keep his medications straight.

While cleaning hadn't been a priority for quite a while, it would never have occurred to her that housework would be Brett's style at all. The kitchen, old and worn as it was, certainly sparkled, though. And if cleaning would keep him from feeding her, she thought, still feeling overstuffed from breakfast, she'd agree to anything. The man was obsessed with nutrition. Hers at least.

She waved a careless hand. "Go to it, Mr. Clean. But not in here or the living room until after four. I'm leaving then for a dinner meeting to make this presentation and I have to get it done. Oh, and don't touch anything on this desk. It may look like a jumble, but I know where everything is."

He took a step forward. "You seem a little stressed."

"I just have to get this done, that's all. Mrs. Barker didn't give me much notice that her husband would be in town."

"Ah. The client from hell."

"He is that. I feel so sorry for his poor wife. She had an idea of what she wanted. Then her husband, whose knowledge of decorating would get lost on the head of a pin, bought some things in Italy about a month ago."

"And you're caught in the middle, which is why the meeting the other day had you so wrung out. Melissa, maybe this particular job isn't worth it."

She shook her head. "This is going to be a showplace. It's like ordering a display window for what I'm capable of turning out."

"But the builder—"

"Is falling into line. Now I just have to finesse the husband. I made some proposed changes to the exterior of the house. They'll lean the house toward antebellum and away from the farmhouse look. It will go just as well with the property and the area since there was Italianate influence seen in nineteenth-century Southern plantations. It's going to work perfectly."

"But now you're under pressure to finish your presentation on short notice. That's stress. *Countdown to Delivery Day* says—"

Melissa sighed. Him and that book! Why couldn't he see that a lot of her stress was about supporting the baby after she was born? And starting a business was like starting a snowball. You had to make it good and solid at its core or it fell apart later. She was all alone in providing for Annalise. He wouldn't be there for broken arms, passing the driver's test, paying for car insurance.

"I'm supposed to avoid stress. I know. I know. But it also says I have to eat tons of food. I have to afford the food before I can eat it. Right? This presentation is an important key to the future and it has to be ready. Now shoo. I have to get back to work.''

He nodded and was gone. She'd expected all manner of distracting noise to clatter through the house but all was silent for the next two hours. Until Brett knocked on the door again.

''Hi, I brought lunch back with me. I picked up Chinese. Sorry it's take-out, but I was on the road.''

''I didn't realize you'd left. Thanks, I love Chinese, but I rarely do take-out.''

''I got to thinking about something I read about so I ran out to a shop at the mall in Waldorf. Here. It's for you. It's a fetal CD player.''

Melissa thought she couldn't have heard right. She laughed, picking up the bag. ''Funny, I could have sworn you said a fetal CD player.''

''I did.'' He took the bag back and pulled out a portable CD player, a set of ear phones and a large belt. ''This—'' he said, gesturing with the belt ''—goes around your hips. It's adjustable and has microphones in it. And the headphones are for you so you can listen at the same time as the baby if you want. The player clips to your waistband. They say classical music is soothing to the baby and reduces stress. I have a whole raft of classical CDs over at the house but I picked up Paganini. Give it a try. This way my cleaning won't disturb your work. It couldn't hurt.''

Touched by his thoughtfulness even though to her it sounded a little silly, Melissa nodded her agreement.

''Great. Here, let me show you how it works.'' Brett picked up the assembly and moved behind her, kneeling on the floor. She could smell his distinctive

KATE WELSH   95

aftershave and his breath on her neck made her shiver
with forbidden delight. Then his arms came around
her and fiddled at her waist with the buckle.

Melissa nearly jumped out of her skin when he
spoke in a deep low tone right next to her ear, "I'll
bring your lunch in here so you can work straight
through."

Melissa watched him go and found herself loading
the CD into the player. She wished she knew what
was going on in Brett's head. Was this the real Brett
that only the loss of his brother and the impending
birth of his niece had set free? Or was it an act?

She'd seen glimpses of this person that night before
Leigh and Gary's wedding. It was one of the things
that had drawn her to him. It was nearly irresistible.
He'd shown an irreverence for the trappings of Bellfield and the airs of his parents' social set that she'd
found endearing, considering his career choice and
custom-tailored clothes. That night they'd met, he'd
kept her laughing with his wisecrack comments and
dancing silver eyes. She had wondered how that humor and smart-mouthed attitude could possibly fit
with his profession.

Back then, in her naiveté, she'd decided it was a
side of himself that he hid from most people. She'd
felt honored that he'd shown it to her, and she'd nearly
given him her virginity in exchange.

The next day, though, the illusions had all come
crashing down around her ears. He'd looked at her
with flat, indifferent eyes and he'd been a mirror image of his father. A man Leigh had confided had a
woman in every city of the world. Melissa was determined to keep her baby far removed from that kind
of influence.

What if he was doing all this to disarm her before he moved in for the kill? What if he'd merely adopted the persona that had worked so well for him once before?

Or was he really this unaccountably charming now that he wasn't angling for anything? She didn't know. And not knowing was driving her crazier than her client from hell!

And why was she so unsettled?

Because if it was his plan to disarm her, it was working all too well.

A Woman's Guide to Housewifery—1930 edition. Brett grinned and kissed the cover before setting the antique book on the server. "Thank you once again, Martha Harris. You're a life saver. You ought to get a Pulitzer even if it's posthumous," Brett told the absent and probably dearly departed Ms. Harris.

Most modern-day Americans—male or female—might think he was being a bit excessive, but the book had not only told him what might need cleaning, it had told him how to clean it. But then again, the average American might not need a cleaning primer. He certainly had. Who knew that laundry soap could create such a sudsy, slippery mess when he used it to clean the kitchen floor? His mistake had served nicely to point out how inept he was at living the lifestyle Melissa cherished. He told himself it didn't matter how different he and Melissa were. This was temporary. His stay here was temporary. He was leaving.

And now the dining room sparkled—and without incident. He looked around. Well, it sparkled as much as it could with paint as old as what was on these walls. There was one thing he'd learned in his progress through the house, and that was how very much this house needed work. While not as bad as he'd first thought, it was bad. Still, he was reluctant to mention it, afraid she'd try making house repairs along with all the rest of the work she was doing. But it worried him. The house needed to look its best.

He decided to tackle her office while she was gone. Once the farm's office, it was the one room in the downstairs she'd redone. Which meant he only had a few months' worth of dust to tackle. Brett stopped as he passed her desk. How could she possibly know where everything was in that jumble? He shrugged. She said she did, so he'd better think long and hard before touching it.

Dust-mopping the gleaming pine-plank floors, the honey-colored paneling on the ceiling and the richly stained woodwork took only a little while. So, half an hour later, he stood once again surveying the mess that was her desk.

Absently he sat in her vintage desk chair trying to decide what to do about the condition of the house. Then he saw the spine of a binder peeking out from under an avalanche of sample books and stray papers. It was marked Stony Hollow Farmhouse. The firm's detective's report had called this Stony Hollow Horse Farm when reporting her inheritance.

He couldn't keep himself from carefully dragging the binder out into the light of day. And he was glad he had. She had so many hopes and dreams for this place. When he'd first arrived, Brett hadn't understood the historical significance of the house or even what the house itself meant to her. Built in the early nineteenth century, the house was apparently so significant she'd done a paper on it in college.

As he read, he learned the house was an honest-to-God Amish-built farmhouse that had only been electrified and centrally heated in the 1960s. The Abells—and Brett had always wondered about that odd spelling—had lived the Amish way of life until Melissa and Leigh's grandfather, Jonah, and their great-uncle, Ed, had left the sect in the forties to fight in World War II.

Looking through the term paper, past the brief family history, he found close-up pictures of nitty-gritty stuff about the house like how its rafters fit together, with arrows pointing out mortise-and-tenons, pegs and the wide plank floors. Apparently the house was a pretty big deal history-wise. So it was a historical house. Living in a historical house would be more acceptable to his parents. If he could get it spruced up. No. Restored!

He thumbed on through the binder behind the term paper and found Melissa's dreams for her family home on paper. Drawings of each room were carefully detailed in color with product swatches and numbers. Brett looked around her completed office. Her dream had apparently ended here. Probably with her uncle's terminal illness, Leigh and Gary's request for a baby and their subsequent deaths.

The crunching of gravel and an odd jangle echoed from the front of the house, drawing Brett's attention. Curious, he replaced the book and went to investigate.

Two Amish men and a boy of about twelve were in the process of climbing down from a horse-drawn flatbed wagon. It was full of shutters like the ones still hanging on Melissa's house. Historic shutters, he reminded himself, seeing a glimmer of light at the end of a tunnel of worry.

When Brett stepped onto the porch all three plainly dressed males stopped and stared at him. "I'm guessing you're what happened to the rest of Melissa's shutters," he said, walking down the porch steps toward them. "Hi. I'm Melissa's—" He stopped speaking abruptly. What was he? Not really her brother-in-law. Certainly not her friend. A would-be lover, but he spent almost all his mental time reminding himself that wasn't possible.

"You are family to Leigh's husband. I see the resemblance," the taller of the two said, rescuing Brett from his active imagination.

The trouble was the man's assertion tugged at his heart, though Brett didn't know why. Trying to cover his reaction, he offered his hand. "Brett Costain. You knew Gary? He was my brother."

"I am Izaak Abramson."

Brett put his age at forty-something. There wasn't a bit of gray in his brown hair but some in his beard. Abramson was about his own six foot two inches and had the build of a runner, though he surely had never worn a pair of jogging shoes in his life.

"Good to meet you, Izaak," he said as the Amish man shook his hand.

"It is good to meet the brother of Leigh's husband. He was a good man and good for Leigh too. I was sorry to hear of his death. It was a very kind man the world lost that day. Last year when rain threatened and my cousins were ill, he helped bring in my hay crop."

This was a part of Gary's life Brett had known nothing about. The idea bothered Brett so he pushed the thought aside. "That sounds like Gary."

"You are here because of the baby?" Abramson asked.

Brett gestured to the dilapidated homestead. "I thought she might need help."

Abramson nodded. "The baby is your family. It is your right. And your duty. You are the one who bought the Jacobs farm. Ya?"

"What was left of it. I thought I should be close." Thinking of the neat, clean Amish farms he'd passed, Brett added, "Melissa's house isn't the only one that needs work. I'm going to be looking for some craftsmen to work on my house."

The man nodded. "This is my brother Od," Abramson said, gesturing to the other adult. As Brett shook the younger man's hand, Izaak continued with introductions. "Od is a fine carpenter. And my son Joseph. We have wanted to paint Melissa's house, but she wants the work on the barn finished and these stables taken down first. They are becoming dangerous."

"Melissa says you're going to make furniture out of them."

"That is the plan. At first I thought she made a joke but she was serious. She often is about business."

"Melissa seems to know what she's talking about."

"As I said she is very serious about this business of hers. She must be, with this baby coming and no father and husband to care for them. Margaret and I do not like seeing our young friend Melissa so burdened." There was no anger in Abramson's voice but a great deal of censure. Brett wasn't sure who it was directed toward. He bristled on Melissa's behalf.

"Melissa was prepared to do something extraordinary for my brother and his wife. I don't like that she's in this position either, but I can't help but be grateful that a part of Gary lives on. Selfish, I suppose, but Gary was my only brother and now he's gone.''

Izaak nodded. ''Perhaps it is not you who is selfish. As good and nice a man as your brother was and as much as I am sure Leigh loved Melissa, it was wrong, this thing they asked of her. Too difficult for a woman to bear.''

Disloyal to his brother though it was, Brett had always agreed. What Leigh and Gary had asked *was* too much. ''Maybe the baby is her reward and not her burden, then. That's certainly the way she feels. At least this way she isn't alone with no family.'' Melissa would at least have the baby, Brett added silently. He would have no one.

''They say God's ways are strange,'' Abramson said. ''Who are we to judge? The Almighty could have confounded English science if He wanted to. Ya?''

Brett nodded and went to help the other two who were unloading the shutters Izaak had repaired. As they worked, Brett asked about workmen he could hire to work on his house and maybe Melissa's. He got names of several other Amish men who hired out doing carpentry and finish work on houses. He also got an idea of how to get Melissa to let him pay for the repairs. The longer the house stayed looking so shabby the more there was a danger his mother would swoop in and create havoc when she learned about the baby.

It was one of the things he had to protect her from. The other was himself and his growing need for her.

Chapter Nine

Brett nearly jumped out of his skin when a booming clap of thunder blasted through his little house a week after he'd arrived back in Maryland and wakened him. A second boom followed a flash of lightning seconds later. He yawned and thought lazily that Izaak had gotten the rain he said he needed.

Absently he reached for the nightstand to check his watch and panic flooded him. Damn. The one day he couldn't afford to sleep in and the skies had conspired against him. The sun usually blasted him awake at just past dawn each morning, but today, when he was supposed to go with Melissa to the doctor, he'd overslept. And it wasn't just the skies that were after him. He'd have been awake if images of Melissa and five-year-old memories of her in his arms hadn't kept him awake into the small hours of the morning!

After dashing around like a madman, Brett drove

his pickup across the road. He maneuvered the compact little truck as close as he could to the porch and honked the horn. But after a few minutes, Melissa had failed to show. Worried, Brett jumped out into the pouring rain, hopped a few deep puddles and trotted up the steps to the cover of the porch roof.

Oddly, a big fat drop plopped onto his head as he neared the door. Brett looked up and frowned as a second and third drip fell on his forehead. It wasn't exactly dry under the porch roof either. He turned back to the door and knocked but Melissa didn't answer. Her car was still in the drive so he knew she hadn't left without him. Which left him wondering if the lack of sunshine had fooled her as well.

He tried the door. As usual, it was unlocked. Still uncomfortable with her open-door policy, with just his head inside her door, Brett called, "Melissa! Hey, Melissa! You awake?"

"I'm up here," she shouted from above. "I hope you meant it when you said you were here to help."

Panic flooded him and he charged up the stairs to the second floor where he'd never gone before. He stopped short at the head of the stairs, almost kicking over a bucket full of water sitting in front of a window. From there two hallways traced the path of the staircase back toward the front of the house. Multiple rooms flowed off each hall with what appeared to be the bathroom occupying the large area at the end of the hallway on the left.

"The trash can in the bathroom needs emptying too," Melissa told Brett as she rushed out of one of the back bedrooms. But he didn't move a muscle. Instead he stood poleaxed and stared at her. The instant the confusion in his eyes mutated to desire, Melissa remembered she was only clad in a bath sheet wrapped sarong-style around her naked body. She felt a blush cover every square inch of her. And worse, she couldn't seem to snag her gaze from the heat in his silvery eyes.

"Don't just stand there," she snapped, finally released when he blinked. *He's the baby's uncle and that's all!* "The roof sprung about a dozen new leaks. The buckets have been filling nearly as quickly as I can empty them. It may as well be raining inside."

That snapped Brett out of his hot-eyed trance. He nodded. "Empty the bucket. Got it. You take care of yourself. I'll handle this."

As she hurried off to get herself dressed for her appointment, Melissa wondered what she thought she was doing. The sky was leaden. Full of rain. There was no way she could rush off and leave this mess behind. She threw on the clothes she'd laid out and vanity made her try to do something with her hair.

When Melissa opened her bedroom door fifteen minutes later, she collided with Brett. Water from the bucket in his hand sloshed every which way, though somehow he managed to keep any from hitting her.

"Oh. I'm sorry," she said, staring down at the puddle spreading around his now-soaking-wet feet. "This day's gone from bad to worse."

When she looked up, Brett grimaced but his eyes sparkled with humor. "It's okay. I was already pretty wet. I'll clean this up too. You all ready to leave?"

She nodded. "But I don't see how I can go. Not with all this."

"Look, I don't need to go today. You do. I'll stay here and handle Stony Hollow Waterfalls."

She started to protest, but Brett shook his head. "Go take care of my niece. I can hold down the fort. I'll still be here for all the rest of the visits. I'll meet the doctor next month. Now go. It'll be okay here."

Melissa didn't have to be told twice. Her appointment was too important. She stopped at the front door and looked back up the stairs, haunted by a thought—one that was quickly becoming a worry. What would she have done without him?

It was better that he wasn't going with her. She was getting too used to having his support and he was only temporary. If only he didn't feel so permanent when she looked at him.

Though as routine as she'd been told it would be, the appointment took longer than she'd thought because an emergency had backed up the doctor's appointments by over an hour. Feeling terribly guilty for leaving Brett for so long to handle her problem roof, Melissa rushed home. She shot up the lane faster than usual and nearly collided with the truck of one of the roofers she'd consulted a few weeks earlier.

The first thing she noticed after he passed her with a jaunty, if soaking-wet salute was a huge bright-blue tarp draping the entire roof and a smaller one that blanketed the section of porch roof over the front door.

"Oh, my God. He wouldn't. Would he?"

Did he think she hadn't carefully considered what to do about the badly deteriorating roof? That she hadn't gotten estimates? Hadn't debated over cost versus historical accuracy? Cost versus getting the shop up and running?

Heedless of the pouring rain, which she was all too

aware was no longer falling inside the house, Melissa ran toward the front door.

"What did you do?" she asked, tears burning at the back of her throat.

Brett climbed down off a ladder. The brass light fixture now shone with a beautiful patina. "About the roof?" he asked, all artless and innocent. "I called a roofer. What else would I do with a roof that's leaking like a sieve?"

"You should have just emptied the buckets the way you said you would."

"The way you've been doing since you got back to Maryland no doubt. I turned on the weather channel, Melissa. This heavy rain is supposed to go on for days. Two early-season tropical storms developed and moved up the coast one right after the other. When were either of us supposed to sleep?"

"But I know how much a roof costs. Do you think I didn't check?" She took a deep breath. She couldn't afford to cave in on this. They came from different places where money was concerned, and he just didn't understand. "Look, I may have been in better shape financially than you originally thought, but I don't have unlimited funds. I planned to do the roof after the barns are down and the shop is ready to open. What are the tarps going to cost me?"

"It's part of the cost for the roof."

"But I'm not getting the roof done now. I can't afford to."

"But I can." He held up his hand forestalling her protest. "No, dammit. I refuse to argue over this. You are not carting water for days on end. Forget it. Think. How tired were you after just a few hours and then multiply that by days? Think about the baby, not finances.''

Melissa squeezed the bridge of her nose trying to fight the tears and waves of exhaustion. How could she let him do more than he was already doing?

''Rebuilding the porch floor, cleaning up the house and helping me keep my head above water around here is one thing. Paying for a new roof—especially one as expensive as the one I plan to use—is another thing altogether.''

Brett didn't say a word. He just crossed his arms and stood there looking big and handsome and stubborn as hell. He did the latter quite well, she realized. And was all the more compelling in this take-charge mode, damn his eyes. The worst part was she knew he was right. She couldn't cart water for days on end. The drought had let her fool herself for too long. The roof couldn't wait.

''Are you ready to listen yet?'' she heard him say.

''Listen? About what? You win. You're right. The roof can't wait. I'll just settle for a shingled roof and replace it later.''

He shook his head. ''This isn't about winning. It's about what's best for you, the baby and the home you intend to raise her in. I know a shingle roof would devalue a historic house. I asked the roofer. And you're right about dismantling those barns. That can't wait either. Neither can the work to create Country and Classics. I have a proposition. Both our places need work. I bought the bungalow knowing it needed a major overhaul. You're an interior designer and in case you didn't notice when you were there for dinner, I need one. Badly.''

''Your furniture is all right,'' she hedged, not wanting to come right out and say what he apparently already knew. He'd wasted his money because that furniture was never going to fit with that house. Unless he intended to double its size.

He shot her a sexy, crooked grin. "Tact 101. I bet you got an *A*. But you can quit being so kind. The furniture's rented from that place in the shopping center near Lexington Park and it looks awful."

Melissa couldn't hold back a chuckle. "I was a little…surprised by the modern leather and glass in an Arts-and-Crafts-style house."

Brett blinked, clearly surprised. "You mean that house has an honest-to-God style assigned to it? Could have fooled me."

She nodded. "It's hidden behind paint and destroyed by modern influences, but it's there at the bones of the building. Arts and Crafts is making a comeback all over the country. The bungalow once had lots of architectural woodwork, stained interior trim and leaded-glass windows that had a simple feel to them." She saw interest mixed with surprise in his expression. "You really didn't consider what you were buying, did you?"

"It was close to you and the baby. I know what I like when I see it, though. And that sounds like something I'd gravitate toward, but I just don't see what you apparently do in that house."

"Trust me, it's a diamond in the rough."

The earnest expression in his eyes drew her like a moth to a flame. "I do trust you," he said. "And that's what I wanted to talk to you about. Izaak introduced me to an interesting concept. He says the Amish barter for services and such. So here's my proposition. I want to barter your talent at decorating for my paying for some of the work your house needs. The roof. Painting. Plaster work.''

The man was incorrigible. ''That's an uneven trade and you know it.''

''I don't know that at all. I paid my decorator on the carriage house at least what the work on your house would cost.'' He named the figure he'd paid and it staggered Melissa.

''You were robbed.''

He shook his head. ''Maybe you undersell yourself. And I'll enjoy trying my hand at painting this place.''

''Do you even know how to paint?''

''No, but—''

''But you can read a book on it and learn how. Right?''

Brett smiled. Grinned really. And Melissa's stomach flipped. Then her heart stuttered. He was so irresistible when he was just being himself. So irresistible he was downright dangerous. If she agreed to his plan he'd be there all the time. That was a downside.

Then again, she'd been wanting to get her hands on the Jacobs house for years and to spruce up Stony Hollow for longer. She just had to continue reminding herself that Brett had made no promises about the future except that he'd be there until the baby came and would return for the occasional visit.

She glanced up at the gleaming light fixture overhead and forced herself to consider the upside again. If Brett kept his word and learned how to paint as well as he did everything else he'd tackled, she'd have herself a bright, pretty place to bring Annalise home to.

Melissa found reason to smile when another thought

occurred to her. If Brett was painting, he might not have time for his favorite new role—diet Nazi.

Melissa wasn't sure what had gone wrong with her plan. In the past two weeks Brett had painted the parlor, the entrance hall and the dining room. All he had left to do was to varnish the woodwork in those areas, and he'd still found time to police her diet and talk her into resting every afternoon.

She'd refused to call them naps. She hadn't even realized how easily he'd manipulated her into those little rests until she'd been visiting a friend earlier that day and heard her say, "Why don't you just go rest on your bed? If you're not tired you won't fall asleep." Her friend had directed that comment to her three-year-old son. Melissa had gritted her teeth. It was the same logic Brett used on her every afternoon.

Brett's footsteps approached her office, and today she was ready for him. "I am not taking a nap. Don't even try to talk me into it."

He shrugged, looking a little crestfallen. "I wanted to know if you felt like sitting on the porch for a while. I can see you're busy, though. It's okay." He turned and left without protest.

He'd had two tall drinks in his hands and had seemed sort of lonely. And sad. Feeling like a heel after all his support these last weeks, Melissa followed him and found him sitting on the swing under the Johnny Smoker tree. The drinks were abandoned on a table out of his reach. He sat staring off into space wearing a downcast expression.

"Want to talk about it?" she asked and sat beside him.

* * *

Brett sighed and looked over at Melissa. She always looked so sweet and good. Since the funereal black she'd worn at the memorial service, he'd never seen her in anything but soft pastel colors. And they suited her as much as the bright jewel tones Leigh had favored did her.

He didn't know how he'd been stupid enough to fall for that sophisticate act the night he and Melissa had met. Her eyes showed her every emotion. And right now they were dark with concern and compassion. The fact that he wished he engendered much different emotions in her didn't take away his gratitude that she was there and willing to help.

He guessed, considering her question, he was pretty transparent to her. Now there was a scary thought. Did she see his desire as easily?

"That obvious, am I?" he asked, hoping the answer was no.

"Sort of. You seem kind of down. I had a feeling it wasn't the plaster problems in the bedrooms."

He shook his head. "I tried not letting it get to me. Guess I failed at that too. Today was Gary's birthday."

"Oh, Brett. I'm so sorry."

Out of the blue, it had struck when he'd opened his eyes that morning. A sudden hollow leaden feeling had come over him. Grief strong enough to drown in. Melissa hadn't been home so he'd called his mother. He should have waited for Melissa.

"Like an idiot I called my mother. She didn't even remember. She said he can't still have a birthday when he's not alive. I hung up on her. I never did that before."

He'd felt so isolated. And not because of where he was but who he was. The son of a cold woman and an indifferent father. No longer Gary's brother. Just Brett Costain. Attorney. Nothing to anyone else in the world. If he died as Gary had, no one would mourn him as Gary's friends and Melissa did. As he did. Other than a few charitable foundations he'd done the legal work for, nothing lasting would be left in his wake. The years of trying to make himself indispensable to his parents, trying to earn their love and attention had been a stupid waste. They could have hired someone to look after Bellfield in their absence. It was more than sobering. It was damned depressing.

He felt Melissa's hand cover his—the skin under her hand tingled. "I'm sorry," Melissa said. "I should have remembered it was his birthday."

"It's the first 'first' without him."

"You know what I think?" she asked him, her blue-green eyes alight with compassion and something he couldn't define. "I think it just stinks! This whole thing does."

"Yeah. It stinks. We used to spend our birthdays together. Guess you and Leigh did too. No matter where we were, we got together. The year he and Leigh got married, he nearly forgot mine. I didn't think he'd want to keep meeting so I didn't remind him or set anything up with him. He remembered the day before and managed to get a last-minute ticket on the Concorde out of New York. He showed up at my hotel in London where I was working on a merger.

"I opened the door all bummed to be alone and he was standing there wearing that crooked grin of his. "Trying to get away with celebrating without me?" he asked as if he'd walked around the corner. We both got drunk as skunks in a pub in the West End, and later Gary ran up a three-hundred-dollar phone bill on my hotel-room account blubbering to Leigh about how much he missed her.''

"He really loved her," Melissa said.

"You know, as much as I miss him, I'm glad he didn't have to live without her," Brett said and sighed. "I'm not sure he could have done it."

"That's probably the most unselfish thing I've ever heard anyone say. I knew him as my sister's husband. Tell me about the big brother he was."

Something surged inside his chest. Something poignant and pure. His love for his brother. "There was never a better brother. When our parents sent us to Aldon, I was terrified. He was too, but he never showed it. The whole train ride he told story after story about how wonderful it would be there."

"Oh, my God," Melissa whispered brokenly.

Brett ignored the horror in her tone and continued the story, needing her to understand where he'd come from more for her sake than in memory of Gary. He knew there was no chance for them and this way she'd understand why. "The headmaster picked us up at the station and started explaining Aldon's rules. He said I would be living on a different floor from Gary since I was only seven. Gary stood up to him and said he believed there had been a mistake. We were to be roommates. Mr. Harkins said that was against the rules. Until I was nine I couldn't be on that floor. They'd consider us sharing a room then, but even that was highly irregular. Gary knelt up on the car seat, fixed Harkins with a defiant stare and said, 'My brother stays with me or you'll have more trouble than you know what to do with.''

Brett chuckled. "I asked him years later what he'd have done if Mr. Harkins hadn't backed down. He laughed and said he'd have cried like a baby. That needing to be strong for me was the only thing that kept him together."

He looked at Melissa and she was staring at him with the same horrified expression on her face. "They put you on a train and sent you away? At seven and nine? And without making sure you'd at least be together?"

Even the scared little boy hidden inside him didn't want her pity. "There are worse places than Aldon. I've helped set up foundations overseas for orphanages full of kids who've watched their parents and siblings die of either starvation or violence."

She blinked. "You have? You know, I just realized I don't know what you do. I know you're an international attorney but I don't know what that means."

He breathed an emotional sigh of relief. He'd successfully changed the subject now that he'd made his point. "I'm not much different from a small-town lawyer. Except I travel a lot, speak more languages and I have to have access to more law books."

She twisted in the seat to face him. "How many languages do you know?"

Later, when Brett realized the sun was heavily into its downward track, he mentioned dinner. They talked on while they prepared it together, ate, then cleaned up. He couldn't recall how she'd done it, but she'd kept him talking. And he'd told her more about his career than he had anyone but Gary. The intimacy of it felt good, but he refused to consider that she'd hold his attention. He couldn't risk Melissa's heart, no matter how much he wanted her. His life—his real life—was elsewhere.

In the last few years, he'd often found himself sought after by wealthy philanthropists who wanted to set up foundations to benefit the world's poor and needy. Brett liked the work but, even more, he liked making sure that the money donated to those worthy causes reached the deserving recipients and didn't wind up lining some middleman's pockets.

Mostly they'd talked about Gary. Now, half a day after seeking her out, he was on his way home to bed, and Brett realized he'd gotten through the day. And he was smiling. She had helped.

Chapter Ten

"Do you play chess?" Brett asked Melissa a week after the waterfall had erupted inside the house. She'd been working nonstop for hours. Since he had a devil of a time getting her to rest in the afternoons, he had taken to distracting her from her work, then suggesting she nap when her eyes grew heavy with fatigue.

Melissa looked up. "Time to distract the little mother?"

Brett grimaced. Well, there ended that ploy. "How long have you known?"

She frowned. "Since the first afternoon. Really, you are *so* transparent."

"Well, so are you. And you're exhausted. So why do you fight it?"

She shrugged. "I've always fought taking a nap even when I was little." A blush crept across her creamy cheeks and she dropped her head on the arm she had on her desk. "Oh. I am so losing it." She looked up. "I think I'll just go lie down and nap like a big girl."

Brett chuckled.

She threw him an annoyed look as she passed. "Smart mouth," she accused.

He laughed and watched her trail through the living room then heard her soft footfalls on the stairs. She had such grace and beauty that it often took his breath away. He could no longer imagine his life without her in it. He wanted her with a passion that was close to paralyzing. Which was pretty sad considering his inability to remain focused on one woman for any length of time. How long, he asked himself daily, would these feelings last?

And then there was her rotten opinion of him. He knew Melissa only tolerated him out of some warped sense of duty to Gary. She was infinitely kind, but he often saw her watching him warily when she didn't think he was looking. A keen desperation that was frightening in its intensity flooded over him.

"If only—" he started to say, but stopped himself with a sharp shake of his head. No, he wasn't going there.

But he couldn't deny that something was happening to him and he didn't understand it. This whole exercise of moving to Maryland was supposed to be about securing the baby's future and getting a chance to be an uncle to her, then leaving and going back to his life. It no longer felt like enough. The longer he was here, the more deeply involved he got with everything to do with Melissa herself.

And the more worried he got. The more he needed her. The more he wanted her.

What happened if there was no room in her life for him? The only way he knew to ensure that she'd agree to let him remain part of her life and Annalise's was to become indispensable to them. And Brett knew that would have to be done carefully, with a walk through the minefield of Melissa's distrust and his own failings as a man. He couldn't let her actually come to care for him without risking her being hurt. All he had to do was continue as he was. She was coming to need him as much as he needed her, even if she didn't fully trust him and—thank goodness—didn't realize how he felt about her.

It would be perfect if she came to like him, but those feelings had to come from something that kept a certain distance between them. He ignored the ache in the region of his heart that thought caused and pushed forward. Melissa was what mattered, not his needs.

Since money had created distance between them all along it seemed wise to let it continue to keep the gulf safely wide, and there was plenty he could do for her monetarily. As he stood in the doorway between her office and the living room, thinking of all the things he could do for her, the sound of Melissa's movements through the upstairs hall echoed through the house.

She entered the bathroom over the front entrance hall and a vision of her naked and ready for a long soak in that big claw-footed tub short-circuited his brain. He pictured her standing afterward with the water sluicing over her creamy skin like Aphrodite rising from the sea. His arousal was painful and instantaneous.

He paced to the front porch and back trying to force

his mind back to the problem at hand. That's when the germ of an idea sprung to life fully formed. He hated the thought of her so beautiful and graceful in that ugly room with its dull linoleum floors and god-awful plastic wall tiles. It was clear Melissa hadn't inherited her wonderful decorating talent from her Grandmother Mildred. The dear lady, who'd added the bathrooms in the mid-1940s while her husband was still in the army, had possessed atrocious taste.

Brett understood that indoor plumbing didn't conform to the historical era of the house but he was sure there had to be a way to bring it into harmony with the rest of the house. The bathrooms could at the very least look a little more cheerful. And he was sure if he'd noticed how awful those two rooms were, Melissa must hate them.

He dropped into the chair behind her desk and his gaze fell on the design binder where she'd recorded all her hopes and dreams for the old farmhouse. It was still buried under several other books on the desk. He'd only glanced at it that day he'd found it. It had been dumb luck that he'd called a roofer Melissa had consulted already or he'd never have guessed she wanted a copper roof like the one that had been on the house before it had been replaced with a modern roof with shingles in the 1960s. When he thought of the sadness in her eyes as she considered settling for a roof that was less than her beloved house deserved, he knew he couldn't take that chance with his newly formed plan for the bathrooms.

Even though he felt a little dishonest, Brett slid the binder out from under the stack. Searching the pages, he found her drawings for the rooms in question. They were perfect. After that, it was a simple matter of using her little copier. And while he was at it, since the kitchen needed updating, by Melissa's own admission, Brett sought out those plans as well.

Redoing the rooms was far and away past their bartering bargain, but it was the only way he knew to show her how valuable he could be in her life while still maintaining a careful distance. A distance he was beginning to hate even as he sought to widen the gap further.

A knock on the front door drew Brett's attention and he raced to answer it before the noise disturbed Melissa. There on the porch stood the infamous sheriff—Hunter Long. Long was about his age and height with sandy hair and shoulders that strained a bit on the white uniform shirt he wore. At the hip of his navy-blue pants was a weapon that to Brett looked like a bazooka, especially since the good sheriff looked not at all pleased to find Brett answering the door.

"Where's Melissa Abell?" he demanded.

Annoyance replaced worry. "Napping. Can I help you, Sheriff?"

"You can tell me what the hell you're doing in Melissa's house."

The guy was supposedly a friend of Melissa's, but he didn't own her. "A little of this. A little of that," Brett replied as he crossed his arms and leaned against the doorjamb.

"Suppose you tell me just who you are."

"Family. And you? Just what are you to Melissa? Her watchdog?"

"Melissa hasn't got any family," Long countered.

"She does now. She's carrying my brother's child. That's enough for me. Her too," he added.

Long moved back a step as if to be able to size him up better. "You're the lawyer."

It bothered Brett no end that Melissa had talked about him to Long but had never done more than mention the sheriff to him as a threat. Exactly who was this guy to Melissa? The sheriff seemed to be a lot more than an old high-school friend.

Brett didn't know why the guy's presence irritated him so much but it occurred to him that his annoyance with Long might very well be jealousy. That was bad. He had no right to feel possessive about Melissa. To prove to himself he wasn't jealous, Brett decided it was time to reverse the growing antagonism between the two of them.

He stepped out onto the front porch and extended his hand to the sheriff. "Brett Costain. And I think we have more in common than our mutual connection to the law, Sheriff. I'd like to think we have Melissa's welfare in common too. Am I right?"

Long paused a moment then shook Brett's proffered hand, seeming to relax. "I try to do what I can. What she'll let me do. She's a little stubborn in that area. I even tried to get her to marry me after Leigh and Gary died, but she insisted she could do this on her own. I don't get why she'd let you help. From what she's said, you and she hardly knew each other."

"True," Brett said, surprised his voice could sound so normal when his mind was in such an upheaval. Long had asked Melissa to marry him? If she'd accepted Long's proposal she wouldn't have needed him at all.

"So how'd you get her to accept help?" Long asked, again bringing Brett out of tumultuous thoughts.

"Until the accident I rarely saw Melissa but, as I said, there's the baby now. So I bought the Jacobs place. I thought the least I could do was move down here till my niece is born and she and Melissa are settled."

Long stared at him for a long moment and nodded. "That's good. She needs someone."

"That was the conclusion I came to when I saw this place. She's napping right now."

"So you said. Let her know I stopped by," Hunter said, and backed toward the steps. "Tell her to call if she needs anything."

"Yeah. Sure. I'll tell her," Brett replied and waved, but silently he added, "when hell freezes over." Nothing could have shocked him more than hearing those words echo in his head. Confused, he sank into the rocking chair next to the door, taking note of his pounding heart and the sick feeling in the pit of his stomach.

Long had asked Melissa to marry him, Brett repeated as he watched the sheriff's car move down the lane. Why was he so surprised? Did he think the entire population of southern Maryland was blind as well as stupid? Had he thought she'd spent the last five years hiding in an ivory tower, keeping herself chaste for the day Brett Costain decided to try for a second chance with her?

Not that he'd even consider asking for such a chance. Theirs was a connection with too many unbreakable ties and he could never hope to be the man she needed. But, for the first time, he realized she was not some miraculously pregnant vestal virgin bound to live out her life in sanctity.

It was clear from the way she spoke of both Joseph

and Ed Abell—her fathers—that she'd been deeply influenced by both men. What happened when she realized Annalise's life was poorer for the absence of such a day-to-day influence? Would she go looking for a husband? And if she found that man, where would that leave him?

And why, knowing what he did about himself, did he want that man to be him?

Shaking his head over the implausibility of her ever turning to him, or of him being able to offer her more than momentary pleasure and lingering pain, Brett went back and retrieved his copies of her sketches. Then he left and went to make at least *Melissa's* wildest dreams come true.

Melissa woke from her nap to a popping, scraping sound coming from somewhere in the distant reaches of the house. She sat up blinking and trying to shake free of the lethargy long afternoon naps always left behind.

What's Brett up to now? She wondered and was soon following the undefined noise down the stairs and along the hall toward the back of the house. It sounded as if someone was tearing apart her grandparents' bathroom. It was funny how she still thought of it as theirs, considering they'd both died back in the eighties.

When she reached the bathroom, the dust and grime floating into the hall told Melissa all she needed to know. But still she found herself asking what he was doing.

Brett turned. "Oh. You're awake. I tried to be quiet. Sorry if I woke you."

"What's going on?" she asked again.

"Demolition," he said, as if taking a crowbar to a bathroom was a normal daily activity for him.

Melissa just stared at him for a long moment wondering why he looked so sensual and masculine with dust on his shoulders and a heavy tool in his hands. Then the import of what she was seeing began to sharpen.

"Doesn't demolishing something usually mean it's going to need putting back together?"

"It will be. I talked to Jerry, the kitchen and bath guy you hired over at my place. He gave me a terrific price."

"Brett, you wouldn't know a terrific price if it walked up and bit you on the—"

"Uh uh uh." He grinned and waved his index finger left and right in front of her face. "No bad words in front of the baby." He glanced down at her stomach and did a double take. "Wow! You're finally starting to look pregnant."

"We had this conversation before. I haven't had a waist in weeks. And stop changing the subject. What do you think you're doing? I never agreed to your redoing the bathrooms."

"You can't tell me you have sentimental attachment to either one of them. The porcelain's eaten nearly through to the iron on every fixture in this room. Since the bathtub upstairs has claw feet and it's in good shape we can use it. It's a lucky break. Jerry says tubs like that are worth a fortune. We decided it's perfect for the upstairs bathroom."

That had been exactly her plan, along with a tongue-and-groove wainscoting on the walls in both rooms and adding a garden tub downstairs. But enough thinking about wild dreams. "I know the bath-rooms look bad but—"

He pointed to the rust-stained tub. "You can't give the baby a bath in that tub. It can't be sanitary as porous as it is and the sides on the claw foot are too high to lean over comfortably. I promise, we didn't decide on anything too extravagant. He has this pro-gram on his laptop. We worked it all out together. Go look at the printouts on the kitchen table."

"This is too much, Brett. I'll never be able to repay you with decorating advice."

"Let me be the judge of how much all the hours you've put in on your drawings and supervising the work on my house is worth. And we haven't even started shopping for furniture. Maybe I'll be hard to please and it'll take days. Go look at the drawings."

Melissa went—just out of curiosity—to have a look, still feeling more than a little overwhelmed. Overwhelmed quickly mutated to thunderstruck when she found the first drawing. She quickly hunted around and found the second drawing—the one for the up-stairs bath. How could Brett and Jerry have nearly duplicated her dream for both baths? She had thought they were unusual, though perhaps in restoration work the ideas she'd had wouldn't be. But how could Brett, who knew nearly nothing about this sort of thing, or Jerry, who did renovations but not restorations, see the potential she saw?

She met Brett in the hall outside the bath and the mess he'd created of it. "I'm amazed," she told him. "Overwhelmed really."

"You like the way they look? Nothing's written in stone. We just thought we'd give you an idea of how nice it could all look."

"I wouldn't change a thing. *If* I were going to allow it," she clarified, trying to strengthen her flagging resolve. "Which I'm not."

"You wouldn't change a thing?" Brett asked, sounding shocked. She guessed since his last attempt at anything approaching decorating had failed so abysmally, that made sense.

"No. It's absolutely perfect. I might have gone a little more conservative on the size of the soaking tub, but—" she said and paused, then continued, trying to sound casual "—but it was only a dream anyway."

"Look, I already screwed up this room so I have to put it back together. And with the pedestal sink and tub upstairs in such great shape, Jerry just has to replace the internals—whatever those are. So the work upstairs will be chump change."

"Brett, your idea of chump change and mine aren't exactly compatible. This could have waited. I could have bathed the baby in the kitchen sink. It's what my parents did with us. But now I guess this at least does have to be put back together. The rest of the house doesn't have to be finished before the baby gets here. Eventually I'll get to the rest."

He stared at her, and she saw the lawyer in him peeking out from under the plaster dust. He still looked sexy. What was wrong with her? Since when did desk jockeys in tool belts turn her on?

"You know, sometimes I wonder who you're trying to convince that you can handle all this by yourself. Me or you?" Brett asked and leaned against the wall with his arms folded stubbornly. "You once warned me that a baby is here to stay and can't be shunted aside. Tell me where the baby is going to nap while men are hammering and banging. You think a construction crew is going to pick the quiet stuff to tear apart while she's trying to sleep the way I did? Napping at least once a day lasts four or five years. I looked it up. You think a crew is going to want to knock off while she takes her afternoon naps? And then there's the mess you'd have to deal with while caring for a baby and running what will really be two businesses.''

Melissa could think of nothing to say. He was right. About more than noise. Who *was* she trying to convince? Both of them, was the only answer. She felt her face heat and cursed her fair complexion.

Brett chuckled, then shrugged unapologetically. ''Tell you what. We'll call it a baby gift.''

''The porch floor was your baby gift.''

''To you. It was a baby gift *to you.* This will be to Annalise. After all this house will be hers one day, right? And you don't really want her crawling over that awful chipped linoleum.''

She had to admit the flooring really had been awful, but he'd already torn a lot of it up and besides why would the baby be crawling in the bathroom? Still, he'd made his point. She could feel her resolve caving. No wonder he was such a successful lawyer. He could argue a zebra out of his stripes. She wondered how many women he'd persuaded out of their clothes. An image of the two of them in the pool house flashed across her mind's eye.

''But this is it. No more. Understood?'' she demanded, banishing the vision of another time, another place in her life.

''Oh, absolutely. This is it. Nothing but this project Jerry and I drew up. You're sure there isn't anything there you'd change? Anything at all?''

"Nothing," she assured him, then on impulse stepped forward and kissed his dust-covered cheek. "You're a nice man, Brett Costain. I think I'm actually starting to like you."

It was a major understatement, Melissa admitted to herself as she retreated to her office, but she wasn't entirely stupid. She might be foolish enough to care for the man, but she wasn't dumb enough to admit it to him. And she wasn't about to let the spark of love she'd once felt for him, the one she'd begun to feel again grow into anything more overpowering.

Because, as many good sides as Brett had, she couldn't forget his history with women. She hadn't been the only woman to succumb to his charms. The others were legion. He was only there because of Annalise and his desire to be her uncle. It had nothing to do with the mother of his niece or any of the momentary flashes of desire he showed for her.

However much Melissa wished it were more, she knew from the stories she'd heard about Brett over the years it couldn't be. And even though she'd truly forgiven him, she'd never forget seeing him with Lindsey Tanner in his arms not twelve hours after her own pool-house encounter with him.

She had to hold on to that memory if for nothing else than to remind her of the kind of women he gravitated toward. They were high-powered, cosmopolitan sophisticates who accepted Brett's kiss-off gifts as payment for services rendered, then faded away to seek out new partners. According to Leigh all of them had remained as unaffected as Brett, and Melissa knew she wasn't built that way.

And there was something else she couldn't forget but frequently did. He was leaving. And every time she felt abandoned or lonely, she had to remember that she was in this alone. After the baby was born he'd leave. And she'd be alone.

Single parenthood seemed more and more daunting the closer it came to that day Annalise would be born. Once upon a time she'd imagined motherhood as a cute cooing baby smiling up at her from the crib patiently awaiting her attention. Now she realized there was a greater possibility of diaper rash, shot reactions and colic in her near future as a single mom.

Not only that but the closer she got to childbirth itself the more she wanted to rethink the entire thing. Every woman she'd ever heard talk about childbirth had sounded like her grandfather and Uncle Ed had when they'd talked about the war. War stories. That's what women told.

Melissa didn't want to go to war. And especially not alone.

Chapter Eleven

"Ms. Abell. The doctor will see you now."

Melissa stood and glanced at Brett who'd made it to the doctor's visit without incident or rainfall this month. "You coming?"

"Wouldn't miss this for anything," he said, and smiled up at her. Melissa's heart tripped all over itself. The man's grin was lethal. Warning signs should be posted when he was near. Beware—Brett Costain Could Be Injurious to Your Health. She took a deep breath, willing her heartbeat to slow. She'd better watch it or her blood pressure alone would give away her growing feelings for him.

Melissa knew she had to face the evidence before her. Guarding her heart against Brett wasn't working. This last week she'd found herself watching him and purposely inhaling his scent whenever he was close by. And the dreams. The dreams were just plain out of hand. Thank heavens she didn't sleepwalk or she just might wake up across the road in his bed one fine day!

Brett followed the receptionist into the examination room ahead of Melissa who had to stop in the hall for her weight, blood pressure and blood tests. She couldn't help smiling as each member of the all-female staff checked their hair and makeup after he passed. Lethal!

She also happily noticed that though he smiled pleasantly back at them, he made no encouraging overtures toward them. But still they fawned. Even the usually serious and all-business Dr. Kantarian was suddenly all warm smiles when she opened the door to enter.

"Well, who do we have here?" the young and pretty obstetrician asked, her dark eyebrows raised in surprise.

"This is the baby's uncle. Brett Costain. Dr. Karin Kantarian."

They shook hands and the doctor said with a wide smile, "I'm so pleased to meet you. And I must say I'm relieved to see someone has stepped up to the plate to support Melissa. Are you planning to be her labor coach?"

Brett took a fast gulp of air. "You mean as in natural childbirth classes and all that?" he asked, his voice betraying only a trace of the panic Melissa saw in his eyes.

"That isn't something we've discussed," Melissa said quickly. She wasn't sure she wanted him there. She was having enough trouble keeping her heart under control where he was concerned. She didn't need to add a bonding experience like practicing for and participating in her baby's birth. She'd be doomed for sure. Talk about intimacy!

"You should discuss it," Dr. Kantarian said. "This isn't something that can be left to the last minute. A class is forming at St. Marys Hospital now. I'm not sure there will be another one starting before you deliver. Or aren't you going to be around that long?" she asked Brett, one perfectly shaped eyebrow arched in challenge.

Brett raised his chin just a little. "I'll be around and Melissa knows I'm ready to help any way I can," he replied, all traces of panic gone from his voice.

"Good," Dr. Kantarian said. "Now let's see how this little one is progressing. Lie back and let's get a look at that tummy."

Melissa had forgotten this part when she'd agreed to have Brett there, consequently, she was just a little taken aback as apparently was Brett.

He frowned. "Maybe I'd better wait outside, doctor. I just wanted to meet you and—"

"Mr. Costain, if listening to the baby's heartbeat makes you uncomfortable, perhaps you'd better scratch your name off the list of possible labor coaches."

"No. I want to be here, but Melissa seems uncomfortable with being partially undressed in front of me. I just didn't want her to be stressed." His eyes shifted and Melissa felt his gaze on her. "I'd like to stay if it's okay."

"Come on, girl," Dr. Kantarian urged. "He'd see more if you were in a bikini."

Melissa looked up. "O-okay," she said, still a little embarrassed. She knew it was only because it was Brett who was there. With Gary she'd have been just fine. She'd never felt anything for Gary but sisterly emotions.

When Brett shot her a grateful smile, she was glad she'd agreed. She just couldn't resist him in any way, and she didn't know what she was going to do about it. It was easy to see the baby meant nearly as much to him as she did to Melissa.

"Well, then. Let's get this show on the road. Melissa, suppose you lie back and we'll try to preserve your modesty."

As Dr. Kantarian helped her rearrange her top and slacks, Melissa felt only a little unsettled. Brett stayed well back in the corner of the room behind the doctor.

"Brett, I'll be using a handheld piece of ultrasound technology called a Doppler ultrasound," Dr. Kantarian said as she squeezed some gel onto the flat polished end of the electronic instrument. "Melissa heard the baby before but I imagine it's still exciting. Now let's see if we can find her. Our girl here has been a cooperative little one so far."

Brett stuck his hands in his pockets and hunched his shoulders as he leaned in the corner deep in thought. The baby was moving around quite a bit and Melissa began to wonder if Dr. Kantarian would be able to catch the sound of her heartbeat. Then a loud swishing sound resounded in the room. Brett straightened instantly and moved closer.

"Wow," he said on a deep exhale.

"Oh! I think she wants to say hi." Dr. Kantarian said and twisted a bit, snagging Brett's wrist and pressing his hand to Melissa's abdomen.

While Melissa's heartbeat bounced all over the place, the baby's remained a steady whoosh. Then

Brett's silver eyes lit with amazement as the baby kicked exactly where the doctor had pressed his hand.

The look on his face was one she knew she'd never forget. Wonder. Joy. Then a poignant wistfulness crossed his handsome features, and she knew he was thinking Gary should be the one sharing the moment. She knew because she felt the same way about Leigh.

A few minutes later, Brett's eyes rose to hers and there was something else written there. It was hot and needy and had nothing whatsoever to do with Annalise. Slowly, as if forcing himself, he pulled his hand away, clearly reluctant to break the contact. The feel of his fingertips gliding over her just before they lost contact tightened her nipples and sent a spiraling shaft of desire through her.

But then she remembered the look in his eyes when the baby kicked and regret replaced desire. She should have shared this with him before. She'd been so busy guarding her heart she had forgotten Brett had feelings and emotions for Annalise that had nothing to do with herself. Melissa just wasn't sure she or Brett could separate feelings for the baby from the desire that had surfaced between them only moments ago.

The pull between them grew stronger. She could feel it. She knew he could too. And though they both fought it and never spoke of it, it grew and grew. She thought of it as a fire, spreading slowly at first then gathering in fuel till it burned out of control. Would they be able to keep the conflagration from consuming their good intentions?

''She's nice and strong,'' Dr. Kantarian said. ''That's what I like to see, Mom and Dad.'' Her big brown eyes widened. ''Oops. Sorry. Mom and *Uncle*. Don't mind me, it's been a crazy day.''

''This is an unusual situation,'' Melissa said, refus-
ing to even think about the vision that had sprung to
life in her mind at the doctor's words. He was never
going to be more to Annalise than her uncle and Melissa knew she had to stop hoping things could be
different. They wouldn't. She was as wrong for Brett
and his lifestyle as he was for hers.

She ventured a glance at Brett, hoping to gauge his
reaction to Dr. Kantarian's faux pas but she didn't get
away with a quick look. Instead her gaze collided with
his and was held captive for a long moment. She refused to read anything into the longing she saw there.
It was physical or maybe even nothing more than that
he wished Gary were there to be the dad in question.

Brett looked away from Melissa and fought to gain
control of his runaway emotions. It was a tough job
with tiny Annalise's heartbeat still echoing in the
room and the sticky gel on his hand reminding him
of that beautiful intimate moment when the baby Melissa nurtured inside her body had moved against his
palm.

He once again felt a surge of desire as the memory
of the moment revived itself in his mind. He wanted
her. It was like a fire in his blood. Everything he did
or thought these days was governed just a little by the
passion he felt for her.

The room went silent as the doctor turned the handheld device off and moved to help Melissa clean the
gel from her skin. The silence should have broken the
invisible connection, but he found it made things
worse. The silence bred an overwhelming void. A
void that reminded him of his life away from Mary-

land. Away from the warmth of Melissa's smile. The heat of her presence.

Ask a question, he silently ordered. Someone had to say something. "The baby sounded okay then?" he asked. "Healthy and...and...fine?"

"Right as rain," the doctor confirmed. "And I'd say Melissa is just fine too," she said absently as she scrutinized the chart. "Okay, Mommy, keep up the good work. Be faithful with those prenatal vitamins and make an appointment for a month from now before you leave. Any questions, either of you?"

Since he'd struggled to verbalize even one question and since the air in the tiny room was growing uncomfortably warm, Brett thought perhaps he should get the hell out.

He unclenched his hand and held it up showing off the sticky gel. "I'll just find a rest room and meet you out front. Okay, Melissa?"

"Great," she said, but didn't look up at him.

He imagined she was even more disconcerted than he was, so he beat a hasty retreat, wondering if his touch had felt as intimate and soul binding to her as it had to him. And had she wished he were a different kind of man as much as he had at that moment?

Unfortunately, he had a long enough track record with women to prove to both of them exactly what kind of man he was. A man just like his faithless, philandering father. It was bad enough his father passed along the rogue Costain genes to him, Brett refused to drag down a wonderful woman like Melissa by fooling himself and her with promises of reform.

Half an hour later, Brett stood in the front entry hall of the farmhouse, waiting for the explosion he knew would come any second. The die was cast. The explosion scheduled.

When she'd left home that morning with several appointments lined up, her kitchen, old and lifeless as it was, had been intact and she'd had no hint of his plans. Though the drawings had been on the table with the others the day he'd directed her to check out the "project's plans," they'd been carefully hidden beneath a pile of tools he'd collected as props. He'd hidden the second bathroom's plans as well, but nowhere near as deeply. As he'd hoped, she'd stopped looking when she came upon those.

That morning after Melissa had left, Jerry had pulled all his workers off the project on Brett's house to help at hers. The men had accomplished a minor miracle. They'd ripped out all the cabinets and had demolished the wall between the kitchen and the old bathroom. In its place they'd framed out a new wall that made the kitchen three feet smaller and gave Jerry ample room for the new soaking tub that now occupied the new space. Even the Dumpster holding all the old fifties-era metal cabinets and the rest of the refuse had been hauled away—a scheduling miracle if ever there was one. But they'd pulled it all off and now it was too late for Melissa to object.

Melissa had been running late, as she'd suspected she would be, when she'd arrived at his place to pick him up, so they'd left immediately with no time for her to stop at home.

Now Brett waited, but no explosion came from Melissa, who'd gone to the kitchen for a glass of water as soon as they'd arrived home. There was just the sound of her quiet steps returning to the entryway.

"Correct me if I'm wrong, but didn't you promise

the plans I looked at would be the last of your little projects?'' she asked, her voice terrible in its reasonableness.

It was going to be harder to dance around her if she was completely calm. He'd counted on heightened emotions to help cover his tracks. He tried to look innocent. ''What's wrong?''

''What's wrong? It's all wrong.''

He charged forward toward the kitchen trying to look outraged. ''Didn't Jerry follow the drawings? I was only gone two hours.''

Brett heard her follow. He nearly sighed when he saw the plans in the middle of the tarp-covered kitchen table. Just as he'd planned. He picked them up and made a production of pacing off the changes. Next was the hardest. He had to feign confusion.

''What's wrong? It looks right to me. But then again, I'm not exactly the authority on this kind of work that you are. Where is he off?''

''What do you mean where is he off?'' she shouted. ''He ripped down the kitchen wall and moved it three feet. And where are the cabinets and the stove?''

Brett blinked, again trying to pretend confusion. ''Melissa, you said the plans were perfect. You said you wouldn't change a thing. I even double-checked with you.''

''I only approved work on the bathrooms!'' she insisted.

''*And* the kitchen. The day I started the demo work on the bathroom you came out here to the kitchen and looked over the plans.''

''Plans for the bathrooms,'' she reiterated.

He shook his head and pointed to a small series of numbers in the upper left-hand corners. ''One of three.'' He flipped to the next. ''Two of three.'' He pulled the kitchen drawing forward. ''Three of three. They were all here somewhere. I thought you knew the garden tub wouldn't fit without the wall being pushed back which meant reconfiguring the whole kitchen space too. Please tell me you saw this third set of plans.''

''No, I didn't. We were talking about bathrooms. I didn't see this. I thought that tub was big for the room but—'' She ran an agitated hand through her hair. ''I can't let you remodel this kitchen to these specifications,'' she added, staring down at the third drawing.

Now came the toughest part yet. He had to look crestfallen which was bound to be tough since her every word played right into his hands. He was helping her in spite of her I-can-do-it-all attitude. ''You don't like the plan? Look, you can work with Jerry. I'll stay out of it.''

''Brett, the plans are perfect. They're nearly the same as my dreams for this room. Except for the wall being pushed in and the addition of the center island, it's my dream.''

''We'll take out the island. Jerry thought it made the room more efficient. But the wall has to stay where it is. The tub's uncrated and hooked up.''

Her deep sigh was all frustration and anxiety. ''Aren't you listening? Why are you being so dense? I love the center island.''

''Then I don't see the problem.''

''You don't—'' She stopped for a deep breath. ''How could you think I'd let you do this much? *Spend* this much. Brett, this is going to cost thousands.''

''But we've been through all this. You agreed it

would be part barter, part baby gift. That having the mess and noise over with before the baby comes was smart.''

"The bathrooms. I didn't see the third set of plans!"

He gestured to the empty room. ''Jerry had the Dumpster hauled away already and they weren't too careful ripping the cabinets out anyway. It's too late to back out now.''

Her eyes widened. "You planned this!"

Uh-oh. He must have sounded smug. And she was getting upset. Damn. "Planned what? The changes? Of course, I did. With Jerry. We drew up the plans. I showed you the drawings,'' he said calmly, retracing the steps. ''They were on the table and you approved them. I thought you'd approved them all. And it *is* too late. Not only did I sign contracts with Jerry, but the wall's moved. The tub is in and the cabinets are gone. Now calm down. Please. I'm sorry as I can be about the mix-up but I can't change what's happened. Look, if it'll make you feel better, you can pay me back.''

"With interest,'' she told him, calmer now.

"Okay. One percent.''

She shook her head as he'd known she would—stubborn woman.

"Four percent,'' she said.

Brett shook his head. "One and a quarter.''

"Three.''

"One and a half,'' he countered.

Now *she* shook *her* head. "Two.''

He felt as if he was playing tennis. "One and a quarter.''

"You went backward!''

"You're arguing too much. My next offer drops back to one."

"You drive me crazy. One and a half percent. I won't go lower."

"All right, but not a penny until the shop is in the black, independent of your design work. Margaret and Izaak are your partners in Country and Classics and I can't let my misunderstanding affect them."

She crossed her arms. "You drive a hard bargain."

He had to fight a smile as he matched her body language and crossed his arms. She had no idea how stubborn he could be. He'd never accept a dime she tried to pay him. He'd just plow it back into the baby's trust fund.

"Remember today the first time she wants to borrow the car or go on a date. Then we'll see where her stubborn genes come from."

She raised her chin in challenge. "I guess we will." Brett watched as Melissa surveyed the room yet again, before she sighed and shook her head. "I'm sure she'll be quite reasonable and accepting of any decisions I make. I'm going to get changed." She pivoted and stalked down the hall.

"In your dreams," Brett shouted after her with a laugh in his voice. He turned, still holding the plans, and looked around the room. "And right out of your dreams," he whispered to the havoc that would soon be replaced by the vision he'd stolen so he could bring it to life for her.

A vision of his own popped into his head. It was of her face—more correctly of the look in her eyes—when the doctor had slipped and called him Annalise's dad. A devastating ache filled his chest. If he couldn't be the man of her dreams, at least he could still supply a few of her other ones.

Chapter Twelve

Melissa heard the now-familiar cadence of Brett's knock on her front door. Since her kitchen and his were both still torn apart after two weeks of sandwiches and take-out, he'd asked her to dinner where they could sit down and eat without the lingering taste of plaster dust. It had sounded like a great idea until he'd made reservations at Solomons Pier.

It wasn't the long drive to the Solomons Islands that bothered her. The food was well worth the trip. The problem was with the restaurant's atmosphere. It was romantic right down to the linens and Melissa couldn't beg off for that reason without risking him realizing how she felt about him.

She didn't know what compulsion made her stop to check her reflection in the hall mirror. She'd pulled her hair up off her neck, though a few wispy tendrils had escaped the loose topknot she'd created. The hairstyle was a little dressy but it didn't look as if she'd done a lot of excess primping. Which she was now guilty of!

Disgusted with herself, she tossed down her lipstick and stared at her reflection. What was wrong with her? Suffering an attack of nerves over dinner with a man she'd eaten nearly every meal with for a month was pure foolishness. Still she couldn't seem to calm her pounding heart or chase away the butterflies that had invaded her stomach.

Really, it was hard enough resisting Brett when he was covered with dust, looking all sexy and rugged, or when he looked endearingly out of place standing at her old stove with a towel tucked in his jeans. He'd be irresistible sitting across from her with candlelight dancing in his eyes, painting his skin with a golden aura, and the moon reflecting off the mirror-calm Chesapeake Bay as a backdrop.

Oh! She was doomed, she decided and went reluctantly to answer the door when Brett knocked again. Once there she took a deep breath, pasted on what she hoped was a serene smile and opened the door.

"You're right on time," she told him with false cheer.

Brett had dressed in a navy jacket, gray slacks and a light gray shirt. His tie matched his silvery eyes to perfection.

Why did he have to be so darn handsome? And that smile he beamed at her was a phenomenon that always melted her resolve. These days his smile always looked spontaneous and sincere, making it impossible for her not to respond to it.

She wondered if Brett knew he'd accomplished a large part of his mission in Maryland. He'd wanted her to forgive him for threatening legal action and she had.

He'd said he wanted her to like him or at least to tolerate him. Well, she more than tolerated him. She really liked the man he'd revealed himself to be in the past weeks.

The trouble was, she was starting to love him as well, however foolish her head told her it was. And that was where he'd failed thus far. He wanted her to trust him and she did where the baby was concerned, but trusting him with her heart was another thing altogether.

"I got directions when I called for reservations, but I may need your help," he told her.

"I've been there. It's a beautiful place and the food's wonderful. But really, Ruby's Diner would have been fine," she told him as she joined him on the porch.

"I'm sure it would have been, but I thought we deserved a treat after eating our own cooking for weeks."

"I've been eating my cooking for years without frequent restaurant breaks. Are you complaining about my culinary talents?"

"Hell, no. Mine."

Melissa chuckled. "You did very well until we didn't have kitchens anymore."

"But I'm always a nervous wreck when I cook until I know it's done and I've tasted it," he admitted, and settled his hand on her back at her waist as they approached the car.

Melissa nearly stopped breathing and her heart tripled its rate when he touched her.

This is not a date. This is not a date, she repeated

silently while shouting orders for her body to cease and desist all craving for his. It didn't listen as usual. And by the time they reached the pickup, even having the physical contact between them broken didn't calm her racing heart or extinguish the need burning inside her.

Directions were soon a blessed distraction but not enough to distract her from wanting to touch the highlights in his hair or from wanting his beautiful capable hands to touch her. Not enough to let her forget how those hands had felt on her body five long years ago. It was as if he'd branded her—imprinted her for only him.

How many men had she dated since then? Three? No. Four! Only the last, Hunter Long, had made it past a few casual dinners. And all because none of them made her feel the way Brett did. Because she'd never been able to imagine them holding her, touching her as intimately as he once had.

Hunter had only lasted as long as he had because he was a longtime friend, and because of all the men she'd ever met, he'd reminded her the most of Brett. Melissa had tried to build a relationship with Hunter but, in the end, they'd both realized that all they were ever going to be was friends. There was no spark. No attraction. No desire.

"Did I tell you how pretty you look tonight?" Brett asked when he opened her door at Solomons Pier. His gaze caught hers. She felt captive and captivating. He seemed just as trapped as she was. Melissa found herself mutely shaking her head no.

"Then I should have."

"There's no reason for you to say such a thing."

"There's every reason for any man who has breath

left in his body,'' he said, then blinked and the spell dissipated. She looked down at the ground and slid out of the seat, unable to decide if he was sincere or just handing her a practiced line.

Because he'd made reservations they were soon seated by the windows overlooking the bay. The sun had begun its descent, setting the bay ablaze with its fiery brilliance. The dining room turned a soft amber, creating an intimate atmosphere. It was everything she'd remembered—everything she'd feared it would be.

"If the food's as good as the scenery, the drive will be well worth it," Brett said, staring out at the water, absently following the progress of a heron's flight.

"If the food hasn't changed it'll be perfect," she muttered, not sure if that would be a good thing or not.

"That's right. You said you'd been here before. A business meeting?"

Did he think she'd shunned the entire male half of the race because he'd rejected her? That she'd run home to Maryland after their encounter and saved herself for the day he woke up? He may have spoiled her for other men so far, but that didn't mean she'd given up looking!

She smiled at him tightly. "Actually, I was here with Hunter. It's where he asked me to marry him."

Brett frowned and looked pensive rather than surprised as she would have thought. Maybe he didn't think she was some modern-day Rapunzel living in her country version of an ivory tower.

"He asked you to marry him?" Brett asked at last. "You never said anything about being engaged. Now or in the past."

"That's because I turned him down."

"Unusual man. I wouldn't think it would be easy to stay friends with a woman who hurt him that way."

She considered Brett for a long moment. When he'd first arrived she was nearly sure he'd have thought Hunter had been given a lucky break rather than been hurt. Perhaps he was changing. She was afraid to hope.

"Most men aren't like Hunter, but there's more to it. We dated for a while and tried to develop something deeper than friendship. In the end, we both realized we were just friends and would never be more. Then Uncle Ed died and Leigh and Gary asked me to have the baby for them. When they were killed, Hunter asked me to marry him because of the baby. Neither of us had found more than what we'd found together, so for the baby's sake he thought we could build a family based on friendship alone. I couldn't let him cheat himself like that and I certainly couldn't put that kind of burden on a child."

Or on myself, she added silently. *Because no man ever made me feel what I did with you—for you. What I still feel.*

Brett studied Melissa for a long moment that was interrupted by one of the wait staff stopping to light the candle on their table and to take their drink orders. After ordering wine for himself and sparkling cider for her, Brett took her hand. Though she sounded sure of her decision regarding marriage to Hunter Long, she still looked troubled. Maybe she was thinking the baby deserved a full-time father. Melissa certainly deserved a man like Hunter Long, but she also deserved a man who desired her and who sparked the inner fire he'd once been privileged to see.

A privilege you threw away, he reminded himself.

For the first time Brett wondered if he'd been a fool that day and not wise at all. As if he were watching himself from far off, he found himself taking her hand. The candlelight flickered in her ocean-blue eyes and she seemed to be studying him.

"Penny for your thoughts," he asked, his voice rougher and an octave lower than he was used to hearing fall from his own lips.

"I was just thinking that you're much different than I thought. More like Gary and less like your father. Do you ever wonder how much genetics plays in the formation of a child's personality and how much environment is responsible?"

At that moment Brett wondered if there was such a thing as ESP and if it was one of Melissa's many talents. Fortunately, he was saved from blurting out too much of his own inner struggle by the arrival of their drinks and complimentary crudités.

Melissa picked up the conversation where she'd left it before the interruption. "I'll bet it was Nanny Annie."

Brett frowned. Lost in a sea of ideas. "What was?"

"What made family so important to both of you. What made you both so generous and caring. It clearly had nothing whatever to do with your childhood or your genes. Or your father's influence either way. Two men more opposite from Marcus Costain I have never seen."

Brett felt lighter than air. She thought he wasn't like his father! No one had ever thought that.

It also sounded as if she had come to like him—

even care for him. What was more astounding was he
no longer thought that was a bad thing. If you wanted
something badly enough, couldn't you make it happen? He hadn't thought of another woman since Melissa had answered the door that fateful day he'd confronted her on her porch.

Couldn't this feeling he got when he saw her—
thought of her—continue for years and even decades
to come? Couldn't he be the kind of man she
needed—the kind he wanted to be? Or would his eye
be caught once again by "his kind of woman" when
he went back out in the real world? The point was did
he want to risk Melissa's heart? If he did, and he hurt
Melissa, he could destroy the friendship they'd built
and lose his chance to be part of the baby's life.

The dinner turned out to be every bit as wonderful
as the atmosphere and as Melissa promised it would
be. Then the waiter asked if they wanted coffee and
dessert on the deck overlooking the bay. Brett was
about to beg off when he noticed Melissa gazing out
over the water. He changed his mind and the night
went from wonderful to magical minutes later when
they settled at a lantern-lit table near the railing. There
was a perfect view of the bay and a soft summer
breeze wafting across the deck.

They sat in comfortable silence for a while, just
savoring the perfect moment. The moon's reflection
on the water painted a silvery path toward the stars
on the distant horizon. The gentle breeze ruffled the
few golden curls that had escaped her artful topknot.
On an open-air dance floor across the deck couples
swayed to a provocative tune about love in the afternoon. Then the rich, mellow sound of Natalie and Nat

King Cole singing "Unforgettable" floated toward them on the breeze, and Brett stood, unable to fight the idea of holding Melissa close.

She looked hesitant to accept the invitation at first then her eyes went all soft and dreamy and she stood, taking his hand. Even with her growing pregnancy more than evident in the soft green dress she wore tonight, her steps were graceful and fluid. He wanted to hold the world at bay and her like this forever. If giving away every penny he had would have frozen time, Brett would have gladly paid the price.

Brett found himself breathing in her scent, trying to capture her essence in his memory. The feel of her silky skin was another sensation he greedily catalogued and stored away for another time. She began to hum the tune then her voice softly joined with the vocalists in a tone that was all the sweeter for being slightly off-key.

They were in the shadow of a patio tree when the song came to an end, but Melissa had already begun another chorus when the last notes died away.

She looked up into his eyes, clearly embarrassed. "Oops. Sorry. I didn't even realize I was singing. I'm always so off-key."

"Sounded just fine to me." He traced her lips lightly with his fingertips. "How could anything this flawless make a sound not fit for the angels? I wonder if my memory could really be right. Do they feel as perfect as they look? Taste as sweet as they sound?" he asked and replaced his fingertips with his lips.

Brett refused to think of all the reasons this was wrong. The reality of tomorrow would intrude soon enough. For tonight he just wanted one unblemished memory of holding her, kissing her, loving her.

Feelings as contradictory as any he'd ever felt in the arms of any other woman surged through Brett. Sweetness and wild desire. Protective and savage. Valiant and afraid.

She was so sweet yet had such fire beneath her innocent surface. He felt protective of her, yet his need for her was savage in its intensity. Knowing he would go to his death gladly rather than hurt her or see her hurt by anyone else, he grew fearful of her power over him. Even with that fear beginning to overshadow all his joy, he could not stop his own exploration of her captivating lips.

But Melissa didn't have a lifetime of yearning and regret ahead of her. She had a well-planned course with the kind of happiness ahead that he'd learned about through her. It would be some other man's arms that would hold her this way in the years to come. Some other man's lips that would caress hers on moonlit nights. And so, when her hands tightened on his forearms and pushed his hands off her hips, he accepted that his few stolen moments of bliss and torture were over.

"It's late," she whispered, and turned toward their table.

"Yeah," he said, following close beside her. "Don't want you to turn into a pumpkin," he added jovially to cover what felt a little too much like heartache.

Luckily, she picked up on his need to lighten the mood. "Are we referring to my shape or a fairy-tale princess's bedtime?"

"Why, Miss Abell, I'm shocked that you would doubt my meaning."

At the table now, she picked up her purse. "I know

what you meant. What I'm doubting is your sincerity.'' Her teasing smile didn't quite take the sting out of her words.

And suddenly Brett couldn't pretend a lightness he didn't feel. The thought of staying no longer felt wrong. But leaving this—Melissa—behind did. ''Maybe someday you won't doubt me anymore.''

''I don't think that's a problem, Brett. Not anymore. If I've learned one thing in these last weeks it's that you're trustworthy.''

Chapter Thirteen

All the next morning and into the afternoon Melissa tried to keep her feet on the ground and her mind on anything other than Brett as she went about the business of life. But it was harder than ever with the memory of Brett's arms around her as they had danced in the moonlight. As he'd kissed her in the shadows. As he'd made love to her in her dreams.

She'd awakened with her covers twisted and damp and had actually reached for him. Finding only an empty pillow that carried the fragrance of store-bought mountain-freshness rather than Brett's musky lime scent had been a rude awakening. A sharp plummet to earth. A dip in icy water.

And so she'd arisen, taken a real dip in cool water in her big claw-footed tub and forced herself to get on with her day. At noon she met with Mrs. Edgar and did a final walk-through on the house on Flora

Corner Road. Next she went to an estate auction and picked up several bargains for Country and Classics. Then she stopped to pick up several sample books at a local drapery maker and dropped them off for Mrs. Barker.

Now, as she pulled into her drive, Melissa found herself looking for evidence of Brett at her house. She felt a keen disappointment that he didn't appear to be there. On entering the house she heard their contractor Jerry speaking to someone in the nearly finished kitchen. Today was the day the counters were supposed to go in and the appliances get hooked up. Decorative touches would be all that was left to do.

She stopped just inside the kitchen door and admired the design and workmanship as another man carted his toolbox out the back door.

"Oh, Jerry, it's perfect!" she told him.

Jerry spun around and smiled. "Brett'll sure be relieved to hear you say that."

"Is he still worried about that little mix-up we had the day you took the old wall down?"

"There was a mix-up that day?"

"Well, not really that day. It actually happened the day he started tearing out the old bathroom. We just didn't realize there was a misunderstanding until later. I didn't see the third drawing, you see."

Jerry frowned. "But I left all three of them right on the kitchen table. They were clipped together."

"Except that the table was a disaster."

"There was nothing on the table but the drawings when I left," he said.

That surprised Melissa though she remembered thinking the messy state of the tarp-covered table was unlike Brett. "Oh, I guess it was Brett who covered the table and had a whole load of tools on it. He must have accidentally covered the kitchen drawing. Still, you'd think a professional like me would have seen the drawing and sequence numbers.''

''I hadn't numbered them yet. You hadn't approved them. Remember?''

Melissa's stomach suddenly felt sick. She remembered that day clearly. Brett had pointed to the top corner of the drawings and said, *One of three. Two of three. Three of three. They were all here somewhere.* Then, *Please tell me you saw this third set of plans.*

She hadn't seen the third drawing because he'd purposely hidden it. Then he'd set out to convince her the oversight had been her fault. How could she have been so blind? Jerry never numbered his drawings until after they were all approved, just in case he had to clarify something with an interim drawing.

She shrugged and forced a smile. ''I guess I don't feel so stupid for missing something that wasn't there,'' she said, hoping she'd covered her roiling emotions. ''Are you just about done here today?''

Jerry eyed the level he had sitting on the top oven rack then gave a screw at the top front of the oven a half twist. ''That about does it.''

''Are you headed to Brett's house then?''

''That's the plan. His kitchen is running about two days behind yours. I guess we'll be seeing you over there more now that the decorating stage is starting up again.''

Melissa doubted she'd ever set foot in Brett's house again, but she acknowledged that she was beyond considering the future right then. She found it hurt even to think about what a fool she'd been. Brett had lied and manipulated her to get his way. And his lie hadn't

been one grasped from thin air in a desperate situation.
That would have been bad enough. No. He'd carefully
planned it all. Setting a trap of words and half truths
for her to fall into. And she had.

"Melissa? You okay?"

Melissa blinked. "Me. Sure. Just thinking. You
have a good day. I'm going up to get changed. Thanks
for all your hard work. It's like watching a dream
come to life."

And another one die, she thought as she turned
away.

Brett was not what she'd thought at all. He was
much more like his father than the image she'd built
in her mind. Leigh's biggest complaint about her fa-
ther-in-law—other than his philandering—had been
the way he manipulated everyone, especially his wife,
to suit his wants and desires. It was exactly what Brett
had done. And he'd led her to believe the mistake had
been hers.

Because of that she'd spent the last two weeks sec-
ond-guessing everything she'd done professionally,
from order forms to specs on her own drawings. She'd
been such an idiot!

Melissa was on her way back down the stairs when
Brett came charging in the front door.

"What's wrong?" he asked breathlessly.

"Wrong? Now what could be wrong?" She sank
down onto a step that put her well above him and as
far removed as possible during a face-to-face encounter.

"Jerry said you were acting weird. There's nothing
wrong with the baby is there? Or with you?"

"The baby's fine. I'm *not* fine. I just found out that
someone I'd begun to consider a friend has been lying

to me. And manipulating me. Making me think I wasn't as on top of my game as I could be. Because of that I've spent weeks doubting myself professionally. But now, of course, I only have to doubt my sanity for not having learned my lesson before this.''

He frowned. ''Who is it? Who would do such a thing to you?''

''You!''

''Me?''

His incredulity only made her angrier. ''Something Jerry said tore the blinders off, Brett. He doesn't number drawings until after approval and after contracts are signed. You purposely removed the kitchen drawing and hid it. That mess on the table was fabricated. What could you possibly use a belt sander, a circular saw or a drill for when you were tearing out the bathroom? Not to mention every size and shape of screwdriver and handsaw known to man. You made a mess to cover up your lie.''

''You'd never have let me do it if I hadn't,'' he defended.

''That was my right. This is *my* house. It could have waited till I had the money.''

''But it needed doing. All my reasons were valid. You admitted it.''

He really didn't get it. And that was what made him dangerous to her and her peace of mind. ''You're right. You presented your arguments and I agreed. So you didn't need to lie and manipulate me, did you? You could have just argued your point with no subterfuge, no tricks, no making me think I'd lost my damned mind!''

''I'm sorry. I never meant for you to doubt yourself.''

"Those were design drawings, Brett. That is my livelihood."

"I was thinking it was your dream. I saw your design book on the house and I wanted you to have what you wanted."

Melissa sucked in a breath, astounded. Even that had been a lie. Brett hadn't shared her vision at all. He'd even cheated there. "Do you even know *how* to tell the truth? No. Don't answer that! I couldn't believe the answer. Just get out."

"Melissa—"

"Out!" she shouted at the top of her lungs. Disappointment choked her. She couldn't even stand to look at him because he looked no different than the man who'd kissed her and held her in the moonlight just last night. She clearly couldn't trust herself to make wise decisions where he was concerned.

"Just go away and leave me alone. Please."

Her voice broke on her last command and she hated it. And she hated him for the tears she longed to shed. Melissa stood, whirled and started running up the stairs in one motion. She just couldn't look at him anymore.

Brett wanted to argue but when she said "please" as if her heart were breaking, he forced himself out the door into his pickup and across the road. He stared at his little house, so changed from when he'd bought it, thanks to Melissa's vision. He gripped the wheel at the top and rested his forehead on the back of his hands, closing his burning eyes. Melissa wasn't the only one whose heart felt as if it were breaking. She was completely right. He could have argued her

around to seeing his point that day. He had, in fact—
just as she'd said.

Had manipulation and lying become that much a
part of him? No. He'd been too afraid of failure to
take the chance. He guessed he wasn't the only one
undermining someone's professional confidence. Arguing was, after all, *his* stock in trade. And he was
quite good at it. Yet, rather than trust his skill and
powers of persuasion with the chance of a refusal,
he'd resorted to trickery.

Brett pushed away from the wheel and slammed out
of his truck, stalking to sit in the shade of a magnolia
tree that afforded him a view of what would soon be
the front door of Melissa's shop. He felt embarrass-
ingly close to tears. The only time he could ever remember feeling this low, other than the day Gary and
Leigh were killed, was the day he'd lost Nanny Annie
and been shipped off to Aldon.

How am I going to make this up to her?

Brett nearly jumped out of his skin when someone
said, "You look like a man with much on his shoulders, Brett Costain." After a quick look around during
which Brett saw a horse and wagon out on the road,
he assured himself that he hadn't lost what was left
of his mind. It really was Izaak Abramson standing
over him in his straw hat and dark clothes.

"I think I made a big mistake," he told Izaak. "No.
I did. I know I did. And I don't know how to fix it."

"If you cut a board too short it is too short. That
is almost the only mistake that cannot be fixed."

Brett stared at Izaak with narrowed eyes. "You
aren't talking about building a house or a piece of
furniture, are you?"

Izaak inclined his head and smiled slightly. "There

is hope for you yet, English lawyer. What is it you did that has you sitting under a tree on so hot a day?''

Brett hadn't noticed the heat now that his heart felt frozen. ''I lied to Melissa. I manipulated her to get her to let me have the work done on Stony Hollow. I had what I guess were noble motives but I seem to have gone about helping her all wrong.''

Izaak nodded sagely. ''This could take some fixing. Only you know if it is worth trying. If it is, you must keep trying. Sooner or later, being a woman, she will tell you how to do the fixing if you do not think of a way by yourself. You might start with a gift of the heart? Maybe flowers.''

Brett jumped up. What was the matter with him? Melissa wasn't the first woman whose hurt feelings he'd needed to soothe. But she was the most important thus far, he acknowledged with a feeling of foreboding.

''Flowers. Great idea. I'll call a florist,'' he said, turning to rush for the phone.

Izaak grabbed him by the shoulder. ''Ones you pick yourself. And while you search for just the right ones to say how sorry you are, think why you are going to so much trouble to seek the forgiveness of a woman who is only the sister of your brother's wife and mother of his child. This should be a gift of the heart, and therefore your heart must understand the gift.''

Brett nodded and watched Izaak stride to the rig he'd left out by the road. Brett didn't need to think about why. He'd hurt her and he was sorry. Very sorry. Izaak's general idea was okay, but he wasn't part of the real world. There were no florists in Izaak's little world. Besides, Brett told himself, he didn't know how to pick flowers. He might pick something poisonous.

Later he felt pretty good about the expensive bouquet he ordered. He'd even paid for Sunday delivery. He was sure that would show Melissa how sorry he was, but it was a long night just the same. When he hadn't heard from her by noon, Brett decided it was time for a more proactive approach. He dressed carefully and started out the door to go to her house.

But the sight in his front yard stopped him halfway across his new Arts-and-Crafts-style porch. There, strewn about, were birds of paradise, orchids, roses and lilies.

Okay. She was even madder than he'd thought. He'd have to think of something else. What did she find irresistible? And then he had his answer, and he could shop for it online. With next-day delivery he'd be back in Melissa's good graces by the very next day.

Jerry walked into the kitchen at three o'clock that very next day with an odd look on his face. "Uh, Brett, I think there's something in the yard you ought to see."

"I thought the porch was done. Is there a problem?" he asked, praying there was. Maybe Melissa would have to handle it and he could see if his second apology gift was any better received than the first.

"It's more a problem with your...ah...truck."

"My truck? What could go wrong with my truck? It's parked in the drive," he muttered as he stalked out the front door and across the porch, stopping dead in his tracks at the sight before him.

"You think it was vandals?" Jerry asked from behind him.

Brett sank boneless to the step at the edge of the

porch and dropped his elbows onto his knees. He didn't even try holding his head up. After all, all he'd have seen was an obscene river of chocolate dripping over the grillwork and onto the bumper. The words *stuff it* formed by fifty dollars worth of melting chocolates decorated the hood of the truck.

The chocolates should have softened the heart of any six-and-a-half-month pregnant woman who craved candy in any form, but chocolate especially.

This was hopeless! How could she reject both his expensive gifts? Then what Izaak had said finally penetrated. Neither had been gifts of his heart. He'd spent no currency on them other than US dollars, a kind of currency Melissa put very little stock in. Maybe he *would* try picking flowers himself.

Three hours later, Brett glanced back over his shoulder at the sad-looking bouquet of flowers sitting in the middle of Melissa's porch in a water-filled mayo jar he'd found in his basement.

While trekking across acres of fallow farmland, Brett came to understand something vital. Melissa was more than Gary's sister-in-law. She was more than the mother of Gary's child. And now he thought he knew why. And why kissing her, being with her, felt so different from his experiences with any other woman.

He'd even found himself wondering if the feelings she engendered couldn't be that elusive thing called love. How ironic would it be if just when he figured out why he reacted to her so differently, he lost her? That he might have lost Annalise should matter more to him than it did at that moment. It was the thought of losing Melissa that hurt and frightened him.

He was a desperate man.

Chapter Fourteen

Melissa opened her door when Brett turned away and walked toward the lane. She was surprised he hadn't left yet another expensive gift. Instead, in the middle of her porch sat a sad-looking bouquet of wildflowers. She felt a little of the ice surrounding her aching heart melt.

It looked as if he'd picked them himself. Arranged them himself.

Did this mean he'd learned something? Anything? Was there still a chance he could be a positive influence in Annalise's life? She was nearly sure there was no hope for him to be more than an occasional visitor in her own life, along with a bittersweet memory of a long-dead hope. The painful tug at her heartstrings made her anger surge once again, and Melissa pushed open the screen door.

''Is there a chance—even a slim one—that you can

be honest about one damned thing with me? Can you take a risk and tell me the truth about something—anything—you've lied about that I haven't caught you at?''

Brett, who'd gotten about thirty feet from the porch, whipped around. He looked at his flowers still sitting where he'd left them, then back up at her. He started back and stopped with one foot on the bottom porch step.

''You want honest? You want truth? You want it risky? Okay. The night before the wedding when you asked if making love was always as miraculous as it was with us, I told you no. That what we were feeling was a miracle. You thought that was a line but it wasn't. I also told you miracles don't happen in my life. That wasn't a line either.

''At the moment I realized you were a virgin I knew I couldn't have you. That I'd destroy you. That I was broken. I still wanted you like crazy, but I stopped us before it was too late. Before I made things even worse. I finally had to face the ugly truth of what I was. What I'd been told I was for years by any woman I got involved with. That I'm a copy of my father. That I'd destroy anyone I let love me.

''I knew in that moment I'd be alone for the rest of my life. Just when I had my hands on exactly what I'd always wanted, I knew I couldn't have it.''

This was a little too honest. Her heart was breaking. ''Brett—''

He held up his hand to silence her and continued, his eyes filled with a burning kind of defeat that was truly painful to see. ''I didn't sleep that night thinking about you. You were the kind of woman who deserves a husband and family and I knew there was no way I could offer you that. By morning I thought I could handle a day of being around you with hundreds of guests as a buffer. But when I saw you in church, I knew I was doomed to be the biggest mistake in your life if I got near you again.

"So I found Lindsey Tanner and asked her to stay at my side and to keep me away from you. There were some things going on in her life at the time, and she took it a little further than I meant for it to go. But then I saw how angry you were, and I knew she'd made sure you were safe from me. So I let you think what you obviously did even though you were hurt too."

Melissa felt a little light-headed, and so she sat on the top step. "You're saying you hurt me for my own good."

"I'm saying I hurt us both for your own good. I know it's too late for us. I knew that was impossible five years ago, but I still want at least to be your friend and the baby's uncle. I'm never going to have a child of my own, but I want to get a chance to be something to some child in my lifetime. To this child."

What did a woman say to a confession like his? She'd asked for some deep risky truth. And he'd given it to her. In spades!

Looking back she could see Brett had been lying about the drawings that day. He'd been a little nervous which, other than about the baby, he never was. She'd thought he was upset by the mix-up but now she knew it had been because he was lying and wasn't comfortable with it.

She looked at him now and saw only a deep heart-felt sadness in his gray eyes. What had those people done to him?

Broken. He thought he was broken. And, tragically, maybe he was.

In a perfect world Brett would have asked her the question Hunter had. Only it would be because he was able to take a chance on the feelings and desires they felt for each other. She could acknowledge her love for him, but he was clearly unable to see that she loved him or to take a chance on loving her in return.

Melissa saw the differences between Marcus and Brett more clearly now than she ever had. She wondered if there was some way to show it to him. That way, even if he never cared for her the way she did for him, maybe she could free him—help him see other possibilities than the lonely existence he anticipated for his future. It was the least she could do to repay him for all his help and support. Besides, she did love him.

Melissa forced herself to smile through her heartbreak. ''I like my new flowers. They really say I'm sorry. The others were gorgeous but…''

He nodded and shot her a sheepish little half smile. ''But I only paid for them. I know. Izaak must be a terrific father.''

''Izaak? You went to Izaak? And he told you to pick me flowers?''

Brett shrugged. ''He sort of came to me and suggested flowers when I told him what I'd done. I didn't understand at the time why he also told me I needed to think about why I was bothering to pick flowers as an apology in the first place. I finally understood a few hours ago.'' He looked down where a rash reddened his arms even as they spoke. ''But I think I was doing too much thinking and not enough looking where I was, though. I'd leave them on the porch table. And maybe not touch them too much.''

''Come inside and we'll wash you up with some brown soap and put some salve on that rash. It looks like poison ivy.''

Brett hesitated. ''I'm forgiven, Lissa?''

He'd called her Lissa. No one else had ever called her that but him and the only other time he had was during their fateful pool-house encounter. And now she knew she'd been waiting all this time to hear it again. ''Forgiven,'' she assured him and stood.

''Contagious?'' he asked, not having moved a step when she glanced back.

''Only if the plant oil is still on your arms or on the flowers. But I must be immune anyway so don't worry. I've rolled in the stuff.''

''Lucky you,'' he said with a self-deprecating chuckle as he went to scratch his arm.

''No scratching. Come on. Let's get you cleaned up.''

It was too soon. Melissa's first natural childbirth class was the next night. And she wasn't ready for that kind of intimacy with Brett after hearing how badly he'd been scarred by life as his parents' son. She wanted so desperately for him to love her enough to take a chance on love. But she feared he would never trust himself. And even if he did learn to trust himself, she was still unsure if she would ever be able to wholly trust him. He *did* have that past of his and she couldn't forget it.

At the toot of Brett's horn, Melissa gave herself one last look in the mirror, picked up the pillows and exercise mat she'd been told to bring and headed for the door. And did it somewhat awkwardly, she had to admit. She could only imagine that was what had Brett springing from the cab of his truck to rush across the yard toward her when he'd been content to beep his horn just a minute or two before.

"Why didn't you tell me you had to bring half the linen cabinet along with you?"

She gladly handed over her burden with a grateful smile. "It's only a couple of pillows and an exercise mat but my arms just don't go around it all."

He glanced at her now-well-rounded stomach. "That's because someone's in the way all the time. Couldn't they supply this stuff?"

She had to laugh at his outrage. "Apparently not."

"Ridiculous. They have a hospital full of pillows. Expecting pregnant women to cart around all manner of equipment," he muttered when he shut her door. It was funny how he got all gruff and grumbly when he was nervous. His obvious nerves about the evening somewhat calmed hers.

Until they approached the meeting room. There were ten other couples of all sizes and races but there seemed to be only two people like her and Brett— unattached. Most of the men stood with their arms around the woman they were to coach or they were holding hands.

The room was one of those stark meeting rooms with cinder-block walls painted with a heavy coat of pastel-green paint. Short-pile, forest-green carpets, several blackboards and a large-screen TV were the only "decor" to speak of.

Brett left her briefly and went to dump their stuff along the wall, then he walked back to her, his hands stuffed in his pockets. He looked unsure and as out of place as she felt. And it must be even worse for him. At least her pregnancy gave her something in common with the other women.

"Hi," one very young and bubbly expectant mother said as she and her husband walked up to them. "I'm Shelly Sue. This is my husband, Bobby," she continued. "The teacher was here a few minutes ago. She just went to pick up a film for us to watch. We're supposed to wear name tags. They're up front."

"I'll go get them," Brett said, sounding a little desperate for something to occupy him.

"I baked cookies. Would you like one?" Shelly Sue asked Melissa as soon as Brett left for the front of the room. Melissa took one and took a bite. It tasted like sawdust but she acknowledged that the problem might be with her own taste buds and not the younger woman's baking skills.

"Your husband's so handsome," Shelly Sue whispered conspiratorially.

Melissa felt her fair skin pink, feeling even more out of place. "Brett isn't my husband," she hastened to explain while he was still occupied at the front of the room writing their names on the tags.

"Not married yet?" she asked. "Oh, don't worry. He'll come around. Bobby here did and he's glad. Aren't you, sweetie?"

"Oh, yes, ma'am. I surely am. I could talk to him for you. You know. Tell him how terrific married life is."

"He's not the baby's father," she blurted out just as the room for one split second went deadly quiet. The bubbly expectant mother looked a bit taken aback, but Brett returned to Melissa's side at that moment, grinning for some odd reason.

He smoothly offered his hand to Bobby, a tall thin twenty-year-old with longish hair on top of his head but with the sides shaved up in a military-like cut.

"I'm actually the baby's uncle," he told the fresh young couple. "My brother was the baby's father. He was killed some months ago so I'm stepping in to help out a little."

Shelly Sue looked appropriately sympathetic and glanced at Brett's name tag where he'd placed it on his shirt. "Oh, Mrs. Costain, I'm so sorry for your sadness."

There were times when Melissa knew she needed a tongue transplant, and as she hastened once again to explain her unique situation, she realized this was one of those times. "Actually, I wasn't married to Gary. He was married to my sister."

"Your sister?" Shelly Sue said, sounding a bit as if she had bitten off too big a bite of one of the dry-as-dust cookies.

"What Melissa is trying very badly to explain is that she had agreed to have a baby for her sister and my brother. They were killed in an accident just after we found out Melissa had conceived for them. She isn't really a candidate for one of those tacky after-noon talk shows."

Just then the instructor, a blond-haired, blue-eyed elf named Kathy Wilson called the meeting to order and asked them all to gather their pillows and make themselves "comfortable" on the floor.

It was a ridiculous request, Melissa quickly realized as she lowered herself to the floor along with all the other roly-poly women approaching their last months of pregnancy. At that moment, feeling awkward and just plain fat, she loathed her instructor—a depressing size two if there ever was one—for just existing in the proximity of Melissa's current girth!

"Labor coaches," Kathy, the sadist, instructed. "It's your job to make her comfortable. Use the pillows, your lap or whatever it takes. If you think this is tough, wait till you're trying to make her comfortable during labor.

"Tonight we're going to watch a film that follows a typical couple through each stage of labor and delivery."

Melissa sat cross-legged on the floor the way she always had before but it bothered her hips so she stuck her legs out straight in front of her. That was good for about two-point-two minutes before it started bothering her back, plus her stomach, which had not looked so enormous on the ride over, seemed to be in the way of true comfort. Next she propped herself on her arms so she could lean back a bit but her arms quickly grew tired.

As Melissa started to shift again, the room went dark and the movie began. Then Brett was suddenly there, moving in behind her, stretching his legs along either side of her hips. He took her shoulders and nestled her back against his chest. It was infinitely more comfortable in one way and caused an infinite number of other discomforts—none of them entirely physical.

She started to sit forward, troubled by the feelings his nearness stirred in her but his hand came back to her shoulder.

"Sh. Relax, Lissa. Maybe I'll get a gold star from our perky little teacher."

It was that name that had her listening. Relaxing. For some reason that name told her she could trust him. That past and future weren't part of that moment they were sharing. That these moments were insular and special.

The film, which took an hour, was as frightening as it was beautiful. They watched the couple go through the various stages of labor, eventually holding their child in their arms.

For her part, Melissa couldn't believe she'd agreed to this! She wanted to renege. Plead for another way to accomplish bringing Annalise into the world. And from the tension in the air, Melissa would have bet she wasn't the only one in the room who felt as she did. There wasn't a sound in the room the whole time the movie ran except for a little squirming as the women grew uncomfortable and moved to new positions.

Melissa had to admit that intimate as her and Brett's position was, she'd never felt more comfortable than she did supported by his strong body.

When the lights came up, the teacher had each of them introduce themselves and tell their delivery date. When she got to her and Brett, however, the instructor did the introducing, explaining their unique situation much better than Melissa had earlier.

They discussed the film and the relaxation techniques they had seen the couple go through, and they all tried one. Then the class was dismissed. It was as they walked to the truck that Melissa noticed Brett hadn't said a word since the film started. Had their position haunted him as much as it had her? Did he regret his offer to be her coach?

There was no time like the present to find out if this was all too much for him. After all, she had no choice. Annalise had to be born, but Brett didn't have to participate.

"Are you having second thoughts? If you are, I can ask someone else to do this with me."

Brett stopped, shock written on his every feature. "I wouldn't miss this for the world," he said, sounding offended that she'd doubt his enthusiasm.

"Oh. I'm sorry. It's just that you've been so quiet since the film. It's obvious that it bothered you."

He nodded and walked around her to the door of the truck, unlocking it. He waited for her to climb in then closed her door before walking around the back and getting in himself. But he didn't start the engine. After inserting the key, he slumped in his seat a little and just stared ahead, leaving her to speculate on the problem.

"Is it that Gary won't be there?"

"Oddly enough, I wasn't thinking about Gary tonight. Not him being gone anyway."

Again he sat in silence.

"Brett, I'm not a mind reader. Come on. Open up. Friends talk about things that bother them. That film has you really troubled."

"I don't understand how she could go through a miracle like that twice and be unaffected by it. Either of them really, but especially my mother. She might as well have given us away. We were little kids and she *gave* us to the school to raise. How messed up is that!"

"Pretty messed up, I agree. When I was fourteen— a year after Mom and Daddy died—a friend of mine was taken away from her mother because she was an addict and my friend was being neglected."

At Brett's look of shock Melissa smiled sadly. "Yes, even here in the boonies drugs can be a problem. I asked Aunt Dora a question similar to yours.

They were very wise people, my aunt and uncle. She said parents are just people who happen to have children. Some of those people can't overcome their own problems for some reason and unfortunately their children suffer the most because of it.''

"And you think—"

"I don't know your parents. Leigh thought your mother travels the way she does to keep the world at bay. She said sometimes she'd see Pamela looking at you and Gary with such longing it broke her heart. But she never accepted any of Leigh's overtures either. Still, Leigh blamed your father for a lot of the distance in your family. For the appearance-means-everything attitudes. Maybe you should talk to Pamela.''

"You're a very nice person. You know that. I did talk to her once. About my father. When I first started at the firm, I heard about an affair he'd been flaunting all over Europe. I couldn't believe she hadn't heard or that she was willing to put up with it. She said she knew, but as long as no one confronted her with his infidelities, she would ignore them. That's when she told me about Nanny Annie and why she'd dismissed her. She said she'd learned then that the price of crossing my father wasn't worth it.''

Melissa frowned. "What did she mean?"

Brett shrugged. "I have no idea. My grandmother came in then. She was my father's mother. She lived with us. Well, I guess technically we lived with her since Bellfield only became my father's at her death. Anyway, Mother clammed up. I could never get her to discuss the subject again.''

It sounded like something out of a nineteenth-century novel—*Jane Eyre* or a similar gothic tale. Melissa shuddered. ''That story needs telling, Brett. Maybe she does hide in her travel the way Leigh thought. Maybe she regrets her mistake in marrying someone as faithless as your father. Her life must be so empty. I think you should make her tell you what she meant that day. If not for her sake, for yours.''

Chapter Fifteen

Brett woke the next morning with his parents still on his mind. It bothered him that his past had gotten in the way of him being able to participate fully in last night's meeting. But he'd been unable to banish the questions that had haunted him for years with regard to his parents. If only he hadn't been so bowled over by the emotions the film allowed to surface.

That Melissa had even noticed his mood with her near future being spelled out in living color before her was incredible. He didn't know how she'd been able to look beyond her own worry and see his mood. Talk about unselfish! She was a miracle. But then hadn't he known that from their very first meeting over five years ago?

He knew Melissa didn't think much of anyone in his family. He was sure she'd only relayed Leigh's idea that perhaps his mother was an unhappy woman with limited choices in life in the hope of making him feel better. But the theory didn't work for him either. Especially knowing how much of a threat Pamela Costain could pose to Melissa and Annalise.

His mother's matter-of-fact threat about making sure the baby, if there was one, was raised correctly, haunted Brett as much as her absence throughout his life had. And as time moved on, he'd begun to wonder if he should tell Melissa that his mother might be a threat. The trouble was, he didn't want to upset Melissa during her pregnancy, especially since it could prove unnecessary after the baby was born. His mother might be so busy with her own shallow existence she'd forget all about Melissa.

As he drank his morning coffee on his newly finished porch, Brett noticed Izaak and several other men driving old wagons onto Stony Hollow's lane. He found himself strolling across the road within seconds, drawn to Izaak and his plainspoken wisdom.

Izaak waved as Brett approached them. "Brett Costain. Come meet Jacob, Henry, Joseph, Paul and William," he said, gesturing to each man. "Have you come to pitch in? We can use all the help we can get."

"What's going on today?" he asked.

"Today the five of us dismantle the old barns. I will be ready for the wood soon and they are dangerous and untidy. Soon we will begin work on the barn that will be Melissa's shop."

With the old barns down, once the trees were cleared for Country and Classic's parking lot, and the winter cleared the bush of leaves, the farmhouse would be visible from the road. He glanced at it. It still looked pretty bad even now that he'd taken down the rest of the shutters.

"I know Melissa wants work to start on the shop, but I wonder if we all pitched in, couldn't we paint the house in one day?"

Izaak narrowed his eyes. "Having this house painted is very important to you. Why?"

"Because I worry that if my parents see the house, they'll draw the conclusion that Melissa is…is, well…poor."

"In your family this would be a disgrace?"

Brett pursed his lips and nodded after a brief hesitation.

"Why would the opinion of such people bother you?"

"It doesn't *bother* me. It worries me, Izaak. I'm afraid they'll see Melissa as a bad parent. I'm afraid my mother and father might take Melissa to court to take away the baby. I don't want to leave it to chance, but I don't want to worry Melissa either."

Izaak nodded. "Then we paint. Samuel," Izaak called to his son. "Take yourself home and help your mother arrange a work day here with as many of our neighbors as will come. Tell her it should be for the day after tomorrow. Tell them we paint this fine old house and make it stand proud once again."

Brett could hardly contain his excitement or his nerves until Friday. The wagons began arriving at just after dawn so he knocked on Melissa's door, waking her. As he waited for her to answer the door, he sent a prayer winging upward that she would be able to accept the help in the spirit in which it was being given.

Sleepy-eyed, she answered his knock.

"Morning, Lissa," he said when she opened the inner door.

She looked like a sleepwalking little girl. Except this little girl was soft and round and as grown-up as they come. And, oh, how he wanted to tumble her right back into her warm bed. His sweet Lissa.

"You're sure up early," she muttered at last, her eyes still heavy.

Banishing unruly thoughts, Brett said, "Everyone is," wearing what he knew was a painfully huge smile. He arced his hand toward the lane and stepped aside to reveal nearly the entire Amish community walking in from where they'd left their buggies on his land on the other side of the road.

Melissa blinked. "What's going on?"

"We have decided your house gives our neighborhood a bad name," Izaak said with a teasing grin from where he stood at the foot of the stairs. "We can stand it no longer. Today we paint this sight for sore eyes."

Melissa's hand flew to her mouth and her eyes filled with tears. "Oh," was about all she seemed capable of saying at that moment. Brett assumed they were happy tears.

"Come, English lawyer. Today you learn to work with real tools," said Od Abramson, who stood next to Izaak. "It is also time for the shop to be made ready for Margaret's beautiful quilts and my brother's fine furniture."

Brett winked at Melissa then followed Od. That was the first he'd heard that the barn work would be done that day as well.

Brett soon found himself laughing and joking with men who'd never even used a telephone let alone a power saw. While in his world these men might have been a subject of ridicule, today he found himself the butt of quite a few good-natured "English" jokes.

As he scaled handmade wooden ladders into the rafters, he felt a little like the Harrison Ford character in the barn-raising scene in the movie *Witness*.

Brett learned more about timber-framing than he'd ever thought he'd want to know. And he found it all positively fascinating. The idea that a man could be part of building a structure and know it would be around for his great-grandchildren's use struck a chord of permanence in him.

That same need to create something concrete in his abstract-oriented career had led him into the work with the charitable foundations he'd helped set up. But this was something he actually put his hands on and watched transform from what it had been to what it would be. It was just plain exciting.

At noon a call went out for everyone to stop work. Confused, Brett followed the men toward the house wondering why they'd knocked off so early in the day. Then he entered the clearing and understood. His disappointment fled. Under the trees next to the house stood several long tables that strained under the weight of large bowls of food that marched down the middle of each. Places were set and the benches lined up along the tables quickly filled. Women served drinks then sat with the children, who had kept all those working supplied with drinks throughout the morning.

Brett saw Melissa in the midst of the women. They were laughing and talking and Melissa looked happy and relaxed. After the meal as the men once again got back to work and fell into a rhythm, Brett took the time to seek her out. He found her on the porch with a couple of young children.

"Brett! Come meet Margaret and Izaak's youngest two children. This is Hanna and this is David."

"Hi, kids," he said, and the little blond-haired girl hid her face against Melissa's shoulder.

"Suppose you go run and tell your mama I'll be along in a minute," Melissa told them. They both ran away giggling as they looked back at him.

"I certainly have been an object of amusement today."

"Oh dear. The men must be in initiation mode. They were like that with Gary the first time he helped bring in Izaak's crop."

"I can't imagine my brother working on a farm."

She chuckled at him. "I would imagine he'd have exactly the same thing to say about you."

He grinned down at her, all soft and sweet-looking nestled in her wicker rocker, her eyes a deep blue in the shade of the porch. She was right. This place had changed his entire outlook on life. Of course, it was more likely the people not the place.

"I had no idea this would be such a community effort. Or that the women would cook lunch."

"So this *was* your idea."

"It was more Izaak and Margaret's. All I did was mention that I wanted to get the house spruced up on the outside before the baby comes and before it was visible from the road. Izaak sent word for her to organize things." He glanced at the beehive of activity going on all over the yard. "The UN could use Margaret's organizational skills. What are the women doing now?"

Melissa grabbed his hand. "Making the baby a quilt. Come see. It's beautiful already."

"Okay, but then I have to get back or they'll be

calling me 'lazy English lawyer' for the rest of the day.''

"I'm sure they're just teasing. Does it bother you?"

He chuckled "Nah. Just took a little while to get used to their dry sense of humor." He glanced back at the pristine west wall of the house. "I hope white with green shutters is okay. I had to get the paint and Izaak said when he'd scraped it and worked on the shutters he could tell those were the original colors. You seemed to be interested in restoring it so I went with those first colors."

She hugged his arm and dropped her head against his shoulder as they walked. "It's perfect."

Brett tried to ignore the feel of Melissa's breast pressed against his arm. He ordered his unruly body not to react, but his jeans were soon uncomfortably tight. "I'm glad it's what you wanted. I didn't know if you'd want their help, but I didn't know how to turn Izaak down either."

"I'm used to this kind of help, Brett. It was the hiring of a contractor to accomplish a minor miracle that knocked me for a loop. This is friends and community."

He smiled down at her. "I'm starting to understand the difference."

Melissa nodded and let go of Brett's arm as they entered the barn where the men were sawing and hammering. The scent of freshly cut lumber now overrode the smell of aged wood and hay that had clung to the atmosphere like a memory of days gone by.

"Izaak and Od decided to use a timber-frame technique to hold up the stairs to the loft space," he explained to her. "Those guys over there are knocking the railings together and those two are handling the actual stairs.''

''Let's go, lawyer. Time to get back to work,'' one of the men shouted from up in the rafters where he was fitting a mortise-and-tenon joint together.

''Looks like my break's over, Lissa. Be careful down here with all this activity going on.''

She watched as Brett snagged one of the taller ladders and climbed up with a huge wooden mallet in his hand. He and Jacob Stolzfus worked together as if they'd known each other all their lives to get the peg in place that would make the timber joint permanent.

Melissa quietly stepped back into the shadows to watch Brett interact with men who lived lives as opposite to the one Brett had lived as was likely to be found in the United States. He threw his head back and laughed at something one of the men below said, then Brett tossed a second peg down at him, bouncing it off the crown of his straw hat and drawing a roar of laughter from several others.

It struck Melissa that if she were to ask Brett at that moment if he was happy he would not look blankly at her as if she had grown a second head the way he had on his second visit to Maryland. Remembering that conversation on rearing children, she wondered if Brett had ever considered any career other than the law. She watched him carefully; the muscles of his arms stood out in stark definition as he balanced on a rafter while pounding yet another peg home with the big mallet.

Yes, he was happy here. And she was happy having him there. For now it would do.

For now.

Chapter Sixteen

Melissa looked around at her beautiful shop and put her hand on her stomach. "It's almost ready for opening day, little one," she told the baby. "Less than twenty-four hours," she finished on a deeply exhaled breath.

"Now that is the sound of a contented woman," Margaret Abramson said as she carried several quilts in the door. "Oh! It looks perfect. You both did so much since I was here last. I love the racks Brett and Izaak made to display the quilts."

"Brett would tell you he only thought of them, but that it was Izaak who figured out how to make them and built them."

"But we are not to brag. The important thing is they are perfect."

Since one of the things Melissa knew nothing about was art, she'd been hesitant to make purchases in that arena. She chuckled, remembering Brett's face when she told him the walls would have to be left plain except for a few antique mirrors she'd found. "It certainly simplified decorating now that I have your beautiful quilts hanging on nearly every wall." Margaret's cheeks reddened and she rushed to put her bundle on the sales counter, drawing a laugh from Melissa. At least someone else around here blushed even redder than she did.

"Where are the little ones?" Melissa asked Margaret, to give her overly modest friend a break.

"With Brett. He was a great help to Izaak with the last of the crop this morning. He rode here with us and took the children off for a surprise."

Brett again. He had put his stamp on Stony Hollow Country and Classics just as he had the farmhouse. Just as he had on her life. It wasn't that he was intrusive. It was just that he walked into a room, and she knew he was there before she saw him. The air between them crackled with a desire she worked hard to ignore. Most of the time she failed.

"He is the completion of you, Melissa," said Margaret. "You are his perfect helpmeet and he is yours. Why do you both ignore such a gift?"

What was she going to do with the whole Abramson clan? From Izaak to Hanna and David, they'd begun to foster Brett as the ideal male to be a father to her child and a husband to her. Melissa had no problem with Brett in the father role for Annalise, but she knew that heartache lay in casting him in any other position.

Melissa propped herself on a high stool behind the check-out counter ready to try once again to explain the realities of the outside world. "Margaret, you know Brett will never be anything more than a friend to me. He has to leave here after the baby is born. He can't put his very important career on hold for us for much longer. I don't understand how he's done it for this long."

Margaret sat on the other stool with her feet tucked primly under her long dress. Her ankles just barely showed under the dove-gray fabric. "You say that because you do not stand aside and watch your Brett watching you. There is love in those eyes he cannot hide from others as easily as he hides it from you and himself. He will not leave this place easily. And he will never stay away."

"If you could see the world he lives in, you wouldn't think that."

"Life, no matter where we live it or how, is not this road or that road with no forks or turns. He is at one such place in his life right now. Soon he will choose where the rest of his life is going. He does not seem foolish to me, and it would be very foolish to leave behind all of this that he has helped create."

"He's a workaholic. He just gravitated to doing the only things he could do to fill his time."

"When Brett first came here, Izaak said he was a very unhappy man," Margaret added, pointing out the window at the subject of their discussion. Brett had hung a tire in a tree between the shop and the house. It was the surprise he'd apparently promised the children. He was pushing David with Hanna clinging like a limpet to his back, her sweet laughter floating in the window on the early fall breeze. "That is a happy man."

Melissa had thought much the same thing a little over three weeks ago. Three weeks? Time was certainly marching forward at what felt like breakneck speed. There were only two more childbirth classes. Tomorrow was September the twenty-eighth and her due date was a little over a month away.

Panic flooded Melissa. "Margaret, I don't think I can do this."

"It will be a fine opening," Margaret said as she covered Melissa's hand, obviously misunderstanding her meaning. "You said you put advertisements in all the local papers and that reporter talked to you on her radio program. The customers will be standing in line!"

Margaret's enthusiasm apparently knew no bounds. Melissa wondered if she could get up that much zeal on the subject of childbirth. "I meant have this baby. The thought of labor scares me to death."

"I have done this five times," Margaret said, and patted Melissa's hand again. "And I have lived to tell about it. It is not my favorite way to spend a day, but I got through it. You will too. I will tell you what my mother told me. Do not think on things it is too late to change. Annalise must come into the world. You must look ahead but—" she held up her finger and continued in a conspiratorial whisper "—not too far ahead. That is the secret. Tomorrow is far enough. Sooner or later childbirth will be yesterday's memory instead of next week's great worry."

It wasn't exactly the pep talk she'd hoped for, but she'd give Margaret's advice a try. What did she have to lose? Hours upon hours of worry?

Melissa took a deep breath. Okay. She would open for business in less than twenty-four hours. And everything had fallen into place with that so far. And though Brett refused to take any credit for it, she knew a lot of it was due to his help. He would help her through childbirth too, when the time came.

Her mood deflated again. But then he would be gone.

Margaret was right. That was looking too far ahead. She had to take it one day at a time.

Brett walked through the back door of the shop around four o'clock on opening day. He leaned his shoulder against the doorjamb and watched the scene before him. With the exception of the four women shoppers who browsed the shop exclaiming over each item they came across and another couple at the sales counter, the scene before him could have come to life from the pages of a hundred-year-old photo album.

The older woman at the register gushed over the workmanship and design of one of Margaret's quilts, while her husband handed over a tidy sum for it. Melissa spent the next few minutes chatting with them as she wrapped the quilt in plain brown paper, tying the package shut with twine exactly the way shopkeepers had for hundreds of years.

Melissa had decided to anchor the advertising for Country and Classics on the passion of her potential customers for times gone by. She dressed in period costume, and, of course, Margaret's plain Amish dress fit in perfectly. An advertising slogan of ''A stroll through Country and Classics is a step into the past,'' had apparently gotten things off to a fine start. Each time that day he'd poked his head in, at least one person had been in line at the register.

''Thank you for coming,'' he heard Melissa say as the older man accepted his package. ''And step back into the past with us again anytime,'' she added with a bright smile.

An old-fashioned shop bell rang as they exited. It really was a step back in time. And appropriate, since lately he'd been feeling a similar phenomenon. Since work began on the building, he'd come to appreciate the simple life lived by the men he'd worked with. It wasn't exactly the life for him, Brett acknowledged. He hadn't lost his twenty-first-century mind. But he'd begun to think a return to jetting all over the world and living his old shallow life would never suit him again either.

''You're having quite a time,'' he said, walking up to Melissa.

She looked so happy his heart ached. And so, so beautiful. The sunlight streamed in the window to her left and shot her golden hair with shining platinum streaks. She simply took his breath away. Why did all the women in their childbirth classes joke and lament their growing size and changing shape? They all, to a woman, had confessed only a few days ago at their fourth class that they felt unsexy and ugly.

He didn't know about the others, but Melissa had never been more beautiful. Nor had her changing shape altered his feelings for her. She was still irresistible to him.

''Things been going okay?'' he asked, hoping to distract his unruly mind and body.

Melissa nodded happily. ''I was surprised you were able to stay away so long today.''

''I've popped in a few times. You've just been so busy with customers that I didn't want to distract you. Today was quite a success.''

''I sold some big-ticket items. Three of Margaret's

quilts, the 1860s blanket chest and Izaak's first barn-wood bookshelf. And, by the way, thank you for the flowers.''

''Even though I bought them?''

She smiled. ''They're perfect. You asked for vintage blooms, didn't you?''

He chuckled and waggled his eye brows at her. ''Somehow I didn't think a vase of millennium roses would go with your theme. And I wasn't about to risk another case of poison ivy by trying to pick wild-flowers again. Do you know Izaak finally confessed that he knew I'd probably get into it? It was his secret strategy. He thought he'd make you feel so sorry for me that you'd forgive me even if the flowers themselves didn't work. Who knew an Amish guy would have such a conniving mind?''

Melissa laughed and the low sexy sound had Brett's throat nearly closing up on him. Her eyes shone as brightly as her hair and her sweetly curved lips called to his.

Hopelessly ensnared, he gave in to the impulse. ''Lissa,'' he whispered as he leaned over the counter and kissed her. Her lips clung to his and drew him in. The world disappeared. Reality took a back seat to bliss.

And then Margaret cleared her throat and said, ''I do believe that a hundred years ago you would now be betrothed.''

''Margaret!'' Melissa gasped and blushed scarlet. She turned away and started fussing with the skein of hemp twine and went automatically into the goodbye speech she'd given countless times that day. ''Uh, thanks for stopping in, Brett. Come back and visit us and step back into the pa—'' she stopped and covered her face.

Brett left laughing, glad he wasn't the only one flustered by that kiss or Margaret's comment. Melissa was quickly becoming an addiction he couldn't figure out how to satisfy. Why couldn't he have been born different?

Brett turned into Shady Hollow Lane and glanced at Melissa. They were on the way home from attending the last of their six natural childbirth classes, and she had been overly quiet all night. And he was worried.

The class was supposed to have been part practice and part celebration, but bad news had overshadowed the room all evening. Shelly Sue Cook, the first person they'd met in the class, had nearly died from a freak complication of something called toxemia. Everyone was badly shaken by the news, but Melissa seemed the worst-hit of all of them.

Shelly Sue was doing a little better, but her baby had been airlifted to Children's National Medical Center in Washington, DC. He was in their neonatal intensive care. The tiny five-pound infant had a good chance, but, like his mother, he still wasn't out of danger. Bobby Cook was currently splitting his time between both hospitals, his job and keeping their aging car on the road.

And now Melissa was scared to death. If he were truthful, Brett wasn't far behind. And he didn't want to leave her all alone in that big farmhouse tonight. Usually, after a class, they both retreated from the enforced intimate contact. He'd just drop her off and go home for a cold shower and a couple of stiff drinks.

Tonight though, all he wanted to do was hold her and make both of them believe that everything would be perfect with Annalise's birth.

Tonight's news had shown him, however, how blind he'd been. He didn't know if Melissa had ever considered that there were still dangers with pregnancy and childbirth in the twenty-first century, but he knew he hadn't.

He'd worried. Sure. But only that something might go wrong with the baby. Never once had he considered that Melissa could fall victim to one of many problems that could occur in the whole process. He realized now that he'd been burying his head in the sand when he'd skipped those chapters describing high-risk pregnancy. That wasn't Melissa, he'd told himself and had closed the book. Now that the door to all those frightening possibilities had been forced open, he couldn't seem to close it again.

He pulled to a stop and got out of the car. Melissa looked surprised when he was there as she opened her door and slid to the ground.

"You're coming in?"

"Yeah. We need to talk."

She nodded and they walked up onto the porch. "It isn't going to happen to me," Melissa said, turning back to face him at her door. "I know it isn't," she said, but there were tears in her voice. Worry in her voice. Fear.

"Of course it isn't," Brett told her, and wondered who he was trying hardest to convince. He took her key and let them in. "You feel like a cup of tea or anything?"

Melissa shook her head and sank to the sofa. She

was turned away from him on the cushion so Brett sat next to her, and reached out to caress her back.

"Shelly has to be all right," she said, and turned toward him. It was the most natural thing in the world to wrap his arms around her and let her curl into him when he saw her face crumple into tears. She cried softly and he knew her tears weren't only for Shelly Sue and Bobby Cook and their baby. She was also crying out of fear for the unknowns of her own date with the mysteries and pain of childbirth.

"What if something goes wrong?" she sobbed.

He took her by her shoulders. "Nothing is going to happen to you. Nothing," he told her fiercely, willing her to believe him. Ordering himself to believe as well. This was why they needed to talk. He had to convince her she'd be fine.

"But if it does," she insisted. "If something goes wrong. You were right. We have to talk about what happens then."

"No! We're only talking about positive things. You're going to be fine. Now stop thinking like this." Melissa shook her head then, and some hair stuck to her wet, flushed cheeks. He reached out and smoothed the wayward strands.

"I have to say this. Just listen," she begged. "If something were to go wrong, I have to know you'll be her father. You have to promise me you'd raise her. Not your parents or any of your nasty cousins. No boarding schools. You. And maybe a nanny. Her…her very own Nanny Annie. Promise me!"

He nodded, not trusting his voice with even a simple word like *yes*. He would absolutely not let anything happen to her. He took a deep breath. "Sh. It's all going to be fine, Lissa."

Once again he gathered her against him in a desperate embrace. "Nothing's going to go wrong. Annalise is going to be born, and you two are going to live in this wonderful old house. You're going to tell her all those great stories about your grandfather and his brother. How they went off to war because a friend was killed at Pearl Harbor. About how they both became war heros. You'll raise her from playpen to high-school homework over at Country and Classics. And she'll go to whatever school she chooses. And she'll be whatever she wants to be. When we're both old and gray and living across the road from each other, she'll visit us and sit while we rock on our porches."

Brett didn't know when Melissa fell into exhausted slumber but he was glad she had, because, though his promises were speculative, they suddenly fell so horribly short of the mark that tears filled his eyes. Why couldn't he share her porch? Her life? Why was he no longer content with the way it had to be?

He closed his eyes and ordered the sadness engulfing him to go away. He was still lecturing himself on his foolishness when he dropped off to sleep. The next thing he knew someone was tapping him on the thigh. He didn't want to wake up and fought off the vague call to consciousness.

He was finally going to get the chance to make love to Melissa and he wasn't going to blow his chance this time. They were in the pool house again but it wasn't the evening before Leigh and Gary's wedding. It was the eve of their funeral. Melissa wasn't pregnant, but he was vowing she would be before the night was out. Neither of them would ever be alone again that way. She begged him not to leave her again. Her soft breath on his face and the soft supple breast beneath his hand had him painfully aroused. And the tapping came again. Harder.

Melissa moaned in protest. Brett opened his eyes and found her blue-green jewel-like orbs staring into his. She flinched as a sharp poke landed on his thigh. He looked down and realized two things simultaneously. The breast in his dream was a real one and the tapping was happening to her as well. He blinked and slid his hand from her breast to the sofa.

''Our girl seems to think it's time we woke up and went to bed,'' he said, and could have bitten his tongue.

Melissa sat up and turned away. ''I suppose. It must be late.''

It was a clear invitation to get the hell out of her house. He decided he'd better take it. To hide his aroused state, Brett stood and grabbed the jacket he'd dropped on the arm of the sofa when he'd sat down to comfort her. Holding it as nonchalantly as he could, he said, ''Well, I'll talk to you tomorrow. If you want we could go see Shelly.''

''Maybe,'' she said, clearly either annoyed or upset.

Then at the same moment as he said, ''I'm sorry about the wandering hands—'' she said ''—you were asleep. I understand it wasn't about me.''

They laughed nervously and Brett headed for the door. But once before she'd misunderstood his feelings for her and the long-ago memory of her eyes filled with hurt and disillusionment stopped his retreat.

He pivoted toward her. ''No, Melissa,'' he said in a voice he scarcely recognized. ''You're wrong. It was completely about you.''

Chapter Seventeen

Melissa sat down on the steps halfway up to her office at Country and Classics. She wondered if she was in labor, but told herself that was ridiculous. Labor was horrible and full of nightmare-sized pains. She still had almost three weeks to go. She'd been crampy and uncomfortable all day, but it hadn't gotten worse. So this wasn't labor. It couldn't be.

Standing a few steps below, Brett frowned up at her. Brett, she'd noticed, had been frowning for two weeks now. He tried to hide his worry, but he was more nervous than she was. She'd gotten to the point where she just wanted it over. Just wanted to hold her baby and see her feet.

"Do you know what I've figured out?" she asked him.

"What?"

"God made these last weeks of pregnancy really

awful so women are thrilled to go into labor. It was a plan. A devious one. I know it. And you know what else? The feminists are wrong. God is a man.''

Brett nodded and said slowly as if pampering someone not quite all there in the head. ''O-kay.''

''I know what I'm talking about. Nobody would wish this on their own gender.''

Brett chuckled. ''A little anecdotal as theories go, but I've got to tell you, I'm buying what you're selling anyway. If a pregnant woman can't speak to that subject then no one can.''

''Exactly!''

Then thinking she couldn't make it up the rest of the steps, Melissa gave Brett her hand and let him help her up. A stronger cramp low on her abdomen hit as she stood. She gasped and sank back to the step, unable to hide her reaction.

''What was that?'' Brett demanded. And she'd thought his perpetual frown was bad! Now he looked like the legendary God of Thunder!

''I've just been sort of wondering if I could be in labor,'' she said absently, trying to remember all the signs of labor they'd been told to watch for. She didn't think she'd had any of them. That woman in the film had cried when she forgot her special breathing. Melissa had been breathing quite regularly all day.

''How long have you been wondering?'' he asked. *Did his voice just shake?*

''Since I woke up. But it's nothing like the film or what Kathy described.''

He looked upward toward her office then back down at the sales floor. In the next breath, she was in Brett's arms being carried downstairs again.

''We should call your doctor,'' he told her.

"But it really isn't bad. At least not till that cramp I just got. I'm telling you, none of the signs of labor she gave us have happened yet. Maybe these are those Braxton-Hicks contractions she warned us about. I don't want to get there and find out this isn't real. I'd feel like an idiot."

Brett set her down on the Queen Anne chair at the foot of the stairs and knelt on one knee next to her. "Lissa, how many people would you say have been born in the history of the world?"

She stared at him. What a silly question. "Trillions, I guess. Why?"

He shot her what she could only call a gentle grin. "Think every one of their mothers had the same five or six kinds of labor symptoms?"

Melissa shook her head. "Call the doctor."

Margaret was so right. All the fear was now yesterday's memory and Melissa sat in bed looking down into the beautiful face of her baby. Annalise's sweet baby smell floated up at her and her seven pounds of little person felt so good nestled against her breast. Melissa's heart swelled with the sheer joy of the perfect moment.

The whole day had been such a miracle. She grinned again and swore her face hurt from smiling so much. But like labor, it was a good kind of hurt.

Not thirty seconds after Brett had gone to call Doctor Kantarian, another cramp had hit. Melissa now knew the cramps had been contractions all along. And she'd been so thankful Brett was with her. He'd been calm and supportive the whole time. He'd panicked a little in the car on the way to the hospital when her two-minute contractions went to thirty seconds without warning, but then so had she.

She looked up at him now, sitting next to her hospital bed. "I didn't know Hunter could change the traffic lights to green from his police cruiser."

"Neither did I. He's got some sort of strobe in his light bar. Thank God he saw us. A couple red lights and things could have gotten a little wild. I don't want to think of delivering Annalise myself. Five more minutes and…"

"Oh, God. I don't want to think about my water breaking in the lobby."

Brett chuckled. "You're blushing again, Lissa."

"You try doing that in public."

"There was only one nice old lady behind a desk. That doesn't count as 'in public.' The Waldorf Mall? Now that would have been in public."

He leaned closer and caressed the baby's soft cheek. "You sure were in a hurry to get your life started, pumpkin. All that practicing and Uncle Brett nearly missed the whole thing."

"You got into those scrubs in record time. I was surprised to see you even though I was trying to wait. I'm sorry you didn't get to help with breathing—"

"You did everything perfectly," Brett said, sincerity darkening his gray eyes. "Including this little sweetheart here. You're the most beautiful baby I've ever seen, Annalise. Just like your mother."

"She actually looks just like *my* mother," Melissa said, wonderingly, hoping he wasn't disappointed that the baby didn't look like Gary.

"Is that some weird kind of postpartum confession? God forbid she looks like Gary. That was one ugly baby," he teased.

"Brett, you're terrible. No baby is ugly."

Brett sat back and grinned. "Hey. Are you doubting me? I've seen pictures. Nanny Annie had to tie a pork chop around his neck so the dog would play with him."

"That is the oldest line in the world. And I know you never had a dog!" she accused, barely containing her laughter.

"Okay, Dad. Out. These two need rest," an amazon of a nurse said as she bustled in closing blinds and tossing towels and hospital gowns in a rolling hamper.

Melissa opened her mouth automatically to correct the nurse's assumption, but Brett shook his head. "Don't," he whispered as he leaned close. "Let me pretend for just a while." He kissed Annalise on her fuzzy head, then captured Melissa's mouth with a heart-stopping kiss. "See you later, Lissa," he said and stood. "I'll be back to check on my girls tonight," he told the nurse and left whistling.

Another miracle. Brett Costain was whistling!

Well two. Any kiss from Brett qualified.

And maybe even a third. Was he starting to see possibilities for their future?

In the distant reaches of his mind, Brett heard the phone ring. Sluggishly, he rolled over and eyed the bedside clock. Eleven forty-five. The room was dark. So it was night. Who would call him at that hour?

Brett's mind suddenly flooded with the events of the day.

Something had to be wrong with Annalise or Melissa! He grabbed the phone. "Hello," he said, and knew he sounded a little frantic. How could something have gone wrong? They'd both been fine when he left them at eight-thirty.

"So you're alive." It was the cold critical voice of his father.

Brett sat up, forcing his pounding heart to slow. Melissa and Annalise were all right. He could deal with his father. "I doubt this is the first you've heard about my leave of absence, Father."

"You left the firm high and dry. You have clients."

"I spoke to my clients. And I left with plenty of notice," Brett said, trying to sound bored. "You may be a senior partner, but the others were all fine with this."

"You're throwing your career away. I'm your father. I have a right to say something about this outrageous behavior. I've been over to the carriage house three times today. Twice yesterday. None of the caretakers have seen you either. What on earth are you doing wherever the hell it is you are?"

Brett tried to collect his emotions but his anger spilled out. "First, it's my career. Second, a long time ago you shipped me off for someone else to raise. That's the day you gave up the right to ask fatherly questions."

"You're beginning to sound like your brother! Aldon was a very positive experience for both you boys."

"You keep right on telling yourself that, but, for the record, Gary and I *survived* Aldon. In the meantime, I have an early start in the morning. Goodbye."

He hung up and sat staring ahead. Why did his father have to call today? Brett didn't want any memories except good ones in his mental folder under October twenty-second. It was Annalise's birthday.

Telling himself to relax, that he was now sure they still didn't know about the baby, that he didn't have to deal with it right then, he lay back down and closed his eyes. He still had time. But hours passed with him staring into the darkness unable to shake the feeling that his parents were a loaded gun and it was trained on Melissa and Annalise. He'd gladly step in front of any bullets it launched. He just wasn't sure how effective that would be.

Brett's premonition of impending doom came true three weeks later. Everything was going well. Annalise was adjusting well to her mother's life as an antique dealer and part-time decorator. She slept almost five hours a night already but middle-of-the-night feeding didn't bother Melissa in the least. She'd even confessed to loving those quiet moments in the dark of night.

Because Annalise took one supplemental bottle a day, Brett gave it to her at eleven each night then kissed both his girls on the tops of their heads and left. That part was getting harder and harder. He didn't want to leave each night and he certainly didn't want to limit his kisses with Melissa to a quick peck.

He'd come to recognize the life he wanted. And that was a life with Melissa and the baby. They were a family and he wanted to claim them as just that. But fear of hurting them held him back. He was sure Melissa still didn't wholly trust him and the problem was he didn't trust himself. He had to find a way to be sure he would be able to forsake all others and remain faithful to her. Maybe, he thought, he should pack his things and return to his world. If he couldn't fight the temptation of other women at least she wouldn't have to see it. But he couldn't seem to make himself leave either.

He arrived home from just such an unsatisfying good-night to a ringing phone. And he knew with a sick certainty it was his father. He even toyed with the idea of letting the answering machine take the call, but knew that was only putting off the inevitable.

"I'm calling to inform you that you've been found out," Marcus Costain said in his stiff aristocratic voice.

"Found out?" Brett asked. There was no sense giving away more information than he was sure his father had and making things easy for him. The more he forced his father to reveal, the better he'd be able to read his intentions.

"The entire office thought you'd just worked yourself into a physical or emotional collapse of some sort. No one suspected what you were really up to. It was quite clever forwarding your calls from the estate to your new home. Though *home* is a bit of a stretch for this…this hovel I'm looking at a picture of right now. You and the little expectant mother look so domestic standing there conversing with your contractor."

"Actually, I've come to appreciate a more simplified life. To my way of thinking, calling Bellfield a home and not a museum is the stretch. Somehow, I think Gary would agree with me."

"That's what this is all about, isn't it? His death has unhinged you. You're trying to live his life. We should never have sent you two away to school together. Separate boarding schools would have nipped that dependency you two had on each other."

"Dependency? God forbid your sons actually loved each other and learned to appreciate the real meaning of family," Brett growled. This conversation wasn't giving him any idea of where his father was coming from except that he was ready for bedlam! "What the hell are you talking about?" Brett demanded.

"That sister of Leigh's. We know you've been with her all this time. And we've obviously found out she did indeed conceive Gary's baby. My oldest son's baby."

"What do you care about his baby? You ignored Gary for most of his life. And tried to make the other half of it miserable. Why the sudden concern for his daughter? She's nothing more than another child for you to neglect."

"I've hired Jonathan Tanner."

Brett's stomach turned over. Tanner was a nationally known custody lawyer. He almost never lost a case.

"That's our granddaughter you and that woman have concealed from us," his father went on. "I will not permit her to grow up with a name other than Costain. Nor will I permit her to be raised in so backward a set of circumstances as the ones the firm's detective uncovered."

So Joe Brennan had got paid for two jobs and had only done one.

"...a back room of a shop for a daytime nursery of all things," his father was saying. "No court will see evidence of the kind of life we can provide and leave the child with a little country shopkeeper. Your mother is horrified. And the very idea that we both accepted Leigh into this family believing her to be from a decent background is simply appalling. Now we find out our son lied to us and that our other son has continued to hide the truth as well as our grand-child.''

''Melissa and Leigh did come from a *decent* back-ground. And no one has hidden anything from you. As I already said. Why would I think you would care?''

''Your mother expressed an interest after the fu-neral. Melissa Abell will not raise that child the way she herself was raised.''

Brett's stomach turned to stone. Was this the way Melissa had felt that day he'd threatened her with a custody suit? If so he didn't see how she would ever come to fully trust him. Unless of course he was able to head this trouble off before it touched her. Then she'd know he could be counted on.

''There is nothing wrong with Melissa or the way she was raised. She is a sweet, kind, intelligent woman with a generous heart and more love for her child than you and Mother ever showed for either of your chil-dren. I'll never let you get your hands on Annalise so that you can do to her what you did to Gary and me. Don't try anything, Father. You'll lose more than a court case.''

Brett slammed the phone down. His father might have cast the first stone, but Brett intended to be the last one standing in this particular battle.

He kept watch all the next day and again the next morning. Finally at eleven a strange car drove in the lane after Melissa had taken the baby over to the an-tique shop. ''Are you looking for Melissa Abell?'' he asked, meeting the woman as she exited her car.

The woman glanced toward Country and Classics. ''I guess I went to the wrong place. Is she over there?''

Brett handed her his business card. "It doesn't matter. I'm her lawyer. I'll take the papers. I was expecting them."

The process server looked surprised then glanced at his card and shrugged. "Okay. That was easy. Have a nice day," she said, and left after handing over the papers.

"So now it begins," Brett muttered, watching the woman drive off. He tapped the packet against his open palm then headed home to look over the charges.

They claimed Melissa was unfit and unable to provide properly for Annalise. That she had agreed to give the child up before she'd even conceived her and therefore had demonstrated a coldhearted, detached set of emotions for the child. Bastards! They were ones to talk about being coldhearted and detached. To allege something like this about Melissa when they'd been in her company maybe three or four times in nearly six years was unconscionable. They didn't know Melissa. Not at all.

They didn't know their son either. Brett grinned and knew he probably looked a little feral and just shy of predatory. And they certainly didn't know how far he'd go to protect the woman he loved.

He hadn't slept much the last two nights, lying awake into the wee hours of the morning. And that was when he'd planned his strategy.

The first step was to head for Philadelphia. Devon more specifically. For a face-to-face showdown. If Leigh's take on his mother was right, she might just be his ace in the hole to keep this thing from getting ugly. And if that failed...

Then he'd get good and ugly. There would be no custody suit.

Chapter Eighteen

Melissa walked into the house with a diaper bag tossed over her shoulder and Annalise tucked against her. She listened, surprised Brett didn't seem to be there. They usually met for lunch and Brett sat with Annalise till she woke for her afternoon feeding. Then he'd change her and bring her to the shop.

"Well, baby girl, it looks as if Uncle Brett has left us to our own devices for lunch and afternoon nap today." She'd come to rely on him so much.

Disappointed more than she wanted to admit, Melissa put Annalise in her cradle and went to see if there were any appealing leftovers. Her message machine was blinking when she entered the kitchen. There were two messages from Mrs. Barker about the wall covering for the master-bedroom closet and dressing area. The second answered the first. Melissa chuckled. Mr. Barker was making his wife crazy.

Then she played the third. "Melissa, you were busy with a customer when I stopped in to talk to you. I have to run on up to Philly. A…ah…a client has a problem I'm hoping I can smooth over. Anyway, I need to give it a good try. I shouldn't be longer than today, but I may have to stay the night depending on who I have to talk to. I'm just not sure. I'll try to get time to call tonight, but I may be back on the road. Give pumpkin a night-night kiss for me and don't wait up."

Melissa's stomach rolled. Something was wrong. She played the message again trying to identify something in Brett's words that could explain her reaction. On the third play-through she got it. He sounded the same way he had when he'd been lying about the drawings. He was lying.

She sat down on the high stool near the center island. What would he have to lie about? Was he going to meet another woman? She closed her eyes as an image of him and Lindsey Tanner rose before her.

No. She wouldn't think that way.

They were a family. He did still hold back some part of himself, but it was the part of himself most difficult to reveal. The part that didn't trust himself. The part he thought branded him as his father's son. It snuck past his barriers each time they kissed, giving her a taste—a glimmer—of a fire so hot she didn't know why it hadn't burned out of control. He wanted her but kept a tight lid on his desire. It was clear he still thought he was broken.

Melissa knew he wasn't, but Brett had to learn he wasn't for himself. He had to learn to trust himself before he could commit to her. She'd see a look in his eyes sometimes. Longing and fear. Loneliness. As if he were right there with her but felt he was on the outside looking in. She'd toyed with the idea of seducing him so he'd face up to his feelings and understand hers once and for all. On the whole, she didn't think it was a bad plan, but she had three more weeks before she could even consider it.

Just as Melissa finished lunch a call came from Jerry. The part had finally come in for Brett's thermostat, which seemed to turn the heater on and off on a whim. He'd known Jerry was stopping by, but he wasn't there and hadn't left his key in the usual place for Jerry to let himself in. Since there was every possibility of a deep plunge in temperatures that night, the contractor wanted to make sure the problem was fixed before they had burst pipes to contend with. Melissa promised to meet him at Brett's as soon as possible.

It was a brisk afternoon, and, after bundling Annalise up for the short trip, Melissa strapped the baby in her car seat and drove across the road.

"I don't know how he could have forgotten," Jerry said when she got out of the truck. "This place is freezing most mornings."

"I guess he was distracted."

Jerry nodded. "He's been acting a little squirrelly since yesterday."

"I hadn't noticed," she said absently, then realized that indeed he had been acting a bit odd. He'd been flitting around like a bee facing an early frost. What was going on with him?

Melissa handed Jerry Brett's key and he took it, but pursed his lips and said, "Listen, I haven't wanted to bother you but I need some advice on that fireplace tile we ordered. I'm not sure it's what you were look-

ing for. Brett wasn't sure either so he wanted me to
hold off. Could you come in and take a look at it?''

"Honestly, why didn't he just say something? He
has to be the most overprotective man on the face of
the earth. I'll get Annalise and be inside in a minute.''

"Okay, meanwhile, if the heater's off again I'll get
it going so the little angel won't be cold while we
look over the tiles.''

"Great. Thanks,'' she called after him and turned
back to get Annalise.

Melissa followed after getting the car seat un-
hooked. She went inside Brett's house and put the
baby, who was contentedly sleeping in her car seat,
on the big deep living-room chair in the warm corner
of the room. As she went to sit on the heavy coffee
table so she could loosen Annalise's snowsuit, her
name jumped out at her from an official-looking paper
that was lying there. A legal paper. She picked it up
and started reading.

In the Court of…St. Marys County, Maryland…
In the matter of the custody of the minor child
Annalise Abell… Marcus Costain and Pamela
Costain vs Melissa Abell. It is alleged Ms.
Abell…

Her heart started pounding. They couldn't do this.
Brett's parents couldn't be suing for custody. She
jumped to her feet, fury overriding fear. They said
she'd never wanted her baby. They wanted to take her
baby. She wouldn't let them!

More important, Brett wouldn't. She knew he
wouldn't. At least not without a fight. But why hadn't
he told her? Why did he have these papers? Then she

realized he'd known for two days this was coming. What had Jerry said? He'd been acting squirrelly since yesterday.

He'd been worried, but he hadn't wanted her to worry. So he'd intercepted them. That was why he'd been so on edge. And he *had* been lying in that message he'd left, just as she'd thought.

She tried to recall exactly what he'd said on the tape. She couldn't recall it word for word, but she hadn't erased it either. Without another thought she went to the phone and dialed home to retrieve the message again.

Soon she was listening to Brett's beloved voice and dissecting the part of his message she'd needed to hear again. *I have to run on up to Philly. A…ah…a client has a problem I'm hoping I can smooth over. Anyway, I need to give it a good try. I shouldn't be longer than today, but I may have to stay the night depending on who I have to talk to. I'm just not sure.* She hung up.

"I guess this would be the problem and I'd be the client," she said, staring at the papers in her hand, pent-up fury boiling her blood. "Funny, I don't remember hiring you, and we sure never talked about you having to defend me against your own parents."

She looked at the papers again and fought against tears. She'd been right all along to worry about those people. Then she rushed back to hold Annalise. They weren't getting their hands on her baby.

Brett looked out at Bellfield's gardens, still colorful with late-fall foliage. When he thought of all the years he'd wasted making sure all this was maintained during his parents' many absences, it made him sick. Not because he'd spent so much effort on the preservation of the estate's beauty or his own heritage but his reasons for doing it. What a fool he'd been, trying to earn the love of loveless people.

So here he was, at nearly thirty-six, finally understanding what was important in life. Thank God, Gary had learned the lesson earlier. At least he'd known happiness before his untimely death.

He checked his watch. He'd been told by his parents' butler—and he shuddered to think he'd once thought having a butler was perfectly normal—to wait in the library for his mother until her friends left. That was her answer to his urgent message.

While waiting, he'd put in a call to his old friend Lindsey Tanner and told her that her father was the lawyer his father had hired. Angry and annoyed at her own father, who she called a mercenary bag of wind, she'd given him one important piece of information. It couldn't have come at a better time to strengthen the "pre-trial motions" Brett had planned for that day. His father had his eye turned toward running for a soon-to-be-vacant seat on the state Supreme Court.

"Brett?" a cultured female voice asked.

He turned from the windows and stared at the woman framed in the elegant doorway. Deborah Freeman, granddaughter of his father's most important client. She'd been his adolescent unattainable dream. Once Miss Pennsylvania, a beauty of unknown limits and talents, she had been as off-limits to the young Brett Costain as the moon. Then she'd married some pro football player and Brett had been forced to admire her from afar.

He held out his hand to her. "Deborah," he said. "I had no idea you were one of Mother's guests. How have you been?"

She glided across the room toward him. It was an obviously well-practiced gait, but still he wondered absently how she floated that way while wearing heels that looked like stilts. Before he knew it, she'd taken his hand and had moved in so close he could smell her perfume—an overpowering scent of some exotic flower. Not the clean fresh-as-rain aroma that seemed to drift gently around Melissa.

Melissa. He missed her already.

"You've been gone so I suppose you didn't hear," she said in her breathy voice. "I've been through a terribly distressing divorce. I heard your mother's butler say you were waiting here to see her. I excused myself and came to find you as soon as it wouldn't be too obvious. Earlier, Pamela said you've been going through a bad time yourself."

Feeling hunted, crowded, as if his personal space had been invaded, Brett dropped her hand and stepped away while trying to make sense of this peculiar scene. "Me? I'm happier than I've ever been," he replied on one level while analyzing what was happening on another.

What was the matter with him?

Here he was with Deborah Freeman offering him his long-ago dream on a silver platter and he felt...well...violated. And an overpowering need to compare his long-ago dream woman to Melissa. The old dream lost on all counts to the real woman back in Maryland with her fresh scent, tousled golden hair and blue-green eyes.

"Are you sure you're happy?" Deborah asked following him—crowding him again. "All I've seen you do is frown since I walked in the room. I remember a different response I used to get out of you."

She ran her index finger down his shirt to his belt buckle. Brett gripped her wrist, pushing her hand away. "Used to doesn't live here anymore," he growled. "My interests have changed dramatically these last months."

"But that isn't what your mother said," she pouted prettily.

Brett fixed her with a steely glare. "My mother hasn't a clue about who I am."

Deborah's eyes widened, and when she spoke, he knew she saw a truth he hadn't been able to see until that moment. "Whoever she is, she's a lucky woman. I'll just head back home before someone realizes I didn't leave right away." She smiled regretfully. "Good luck, Brett. Have a good life."

"Thanks," Brett said, and watched in amazement as she glided out of the room. At that moment the truth of what she'd said finally hit him. Temptation! She should have been a wonderful, glorious temptation. And he hadn't even been interested, let alone tempted.

And all because she wasn't Melissa. The woman he loved. The woman he'd have no trouble remaining faithful to. The woman he hadn't even been tempted to cheat on!

Ten minutes later, Brett was still waiting for his mother when he remembered that Jerry was supposed to meet him at his house to fix the heater. Then he relaxed. Jerry would just get the key from Melissa or ask her to open the house for him.

Stark terror invaded his heart then. What if she saw the notice? Would she think he'd been spying on her all along? Conspiring with them against her?

Why had he even left it behind? Because he'd been so sure he could force his parents to back down. The only thing he could do now was call Jerry. It didn't take long for the contractor to answer his cell phone. "Jerry, it's Brett Costain."

"Man, where were you? I had to bother Melissa to open the door for me. I felt terrible for making her come over here with the baby and all."

"Did she unlock the door then head back to the shop?"

"Not right away, no. I figured since she was here and we wanted her opinion on those fireplace tiles I'd ask her to come on in."

"Did that go okay?"

"Funny thing. When I got back upstairs after manually firing up the heater, she said she had to go. Maybe it was too cold in here for the little angel. Melissa seemed kind of worried all of a sudden."

"Yeah. That must be it," Brett said, but he had a sinking feeling the temperature hadn't been it at all. "Listen, I think I left a bunch of papers on the cocktail table. Could you see if they're there?"

"No, man. Sorry. There's nothing there but the baby's pacifier."

"Damn," Brett groaned.

"You okay?" Jerry asked.

"Yeah, if I have anything to say about it by the end of the day it won't matter anyway. Thanks. Sorry I had to leave you in a lurch."

"No problem. Just take care of business and get on back here. Your girls need you here."

Brett closed his eyes after hanging up and willed her to hear him across the miles that separated them. "Please believe in me, Lissa," he whispered. He was tempted to call her. But what could he say? "Don't worry. I'm fixing it." She'd worry anyway, and if she believed him guilty of collusion it would be too easy for her to refuse to listen. He couldn't forget the sight of those chocolates melting on his hood.

More anxious than ever to get this business handled so he could get back to Melissa and Annalise, Brett went to find his mother. He'd waited long enough.

He only hoped he hadn't waited too long.

Chapter Nineteen

Brett found his mother in the conservatory and she was alone. No guests to be seen. "Did you forget about me when your friends left or are you just avoiding me?" he demanded without preliminary.

Pamela Costain was standing near the wet bar. She hurriedly put her glass down and turned toward him, her hand over her heart. "Good God, Brett, you scared the life out of me!"

He dipped his head slightly. "My apologies," he said stiffly. "Now please answer my question."

His mother appeared a bit more unnerved than he'd expected, though she tried to hide her nervousness with motion. She flitted toward him across the bright, glass-walled room and sat on the settee then indicated that he should join her on its mate across from her. She was a beautiful woman, but her beauty was practiced and choreographed to perfection, unlike that of

Melissa, who'd looked beautiful in labor, with dirt on her face as she'd planted mums in the garden around her shop or even standing sleepy-eyed at her front door the morning he'd awakened her with his repair work on her porch.

"This entire matter isn't easy for me," his mother replied. "You must know I don't do it lightly. Though I would think if you've grown attached to the child, our having her here will give you better access."

Didn't the woman have a feeling bone in her body? Brett felt as if his head were going to explode. Well, at least she hadn't pretended not to understand why he was there, he consoled himself.

Having regained some semblance of calm, but with sarcasm still thick in his voice he asked, "Grown attached?"

"To the baby, dear. I don't share your father's opinion that you've lost your mind. I know if Melissa is anything it's a passing fancy. You'll just replace her soon enough."

Brett decided to leave the subject of Melissa alone for the moment. Perhaps his mother could grasp the reason for his interest in Annalise's future. "Of course I've grown attached to the baby. I love her. I did before she was even born."

"There, you see how wonderfully this will work out."

No. Apparently she didn't understand that there was someone else involved in this other than the high-and-mighty Costains and their wants and desires. Incredible!

"Wonderfully? It will work out wonderfully? Tell me, Mother, how wonderful do you think it would be for Melissa to have her child snatched away?"

"It is *Gary's* child."

"Gary would have been her father. I have no doubt he'd have been a good one, but he never had the chance. Melissa has been that child's mother since Annalise was conceived."

"She agreed to give it away. How much could it matter? It was Gary's."

"*It* has a name. Annalise. Melissa agreed to let Leigh and Gary raise her. It was a beautiful, selfless act. And now that selfless act is being corrupted by you and my father and his hired gun. Two of the parties who entered into that verbal agreement are now gone. Melissa is the third. There still needed to be a formal adoption where she'd have signed over her rights. That never took place."

"I don't care!" his mother shouted, her voice brittle and splintered.

Brett had never heard her raise her voice so much as an octave. She was really emotional about this. Maybe Leigh had been right about his mother. Maybe it was time to get to the heart of the matter. Perhaps suppressed feelings were at the heart of her emotional outburst, and he could appeal to her on that level.

He studied her for a moment longer. "Tell me something. Why do you want to steal another woman's child when you never wanted your own?"

Her back stiffened. "You know nothing about my feelings or desires for my children."

Brett cast her a look of disbelief. "Don't you find that odd? Me being one of them and all? Do you even know what it means to selflessly love your child?"

Pamela Costain jumped up, agitated. "Yes, I know. I loved my little boys."

Brett refused to let her ruffled state affect his plan

of attack or notch up his own emotions, which were hanging on the hairy edge of explosion. He twisted in his seat and leaned back, crossing his ankles. "Then you had an odd way of showing it."

"I did what I thought at the time was best. It's all any parent does."

"Why did you send Nanny Annie away? We were relatively happy till then. Why did you send us to Aldon?"

"Marcus left me no choice about Annie."

"Because he tried to seduce her and you couldn't abide having her around."

She'd been pacing and turned back to him, her eyes suddenly burning with anger. "I never wanted that woman here. *They* brought her. Marcus and his mother, that witch, Angelique. I had either to do as they said or lose you both altogether."

Brett narrowed his eyes. Was she telling the truth? It was a version he'd never heard. Of course he'd only assumed Annie had been there for his mother's convenience. "Grandmother and Father hired Annie?"

"If you'll recall, I was allowed to see you at meals and for an hour in the evenings, but even then they interfered. *She* had to be there."

"Allowed? Why do you say allowed? I thought that was all the time you had for us."

"Allowed," she reiterated and sank back down to the brightly flowered settee across from him. "I made a mistake. Because I—I drank." She closed her eyes for a long second. "There. It's said."

"You don't drink overly much."

"Oh, my dear boy, I've been drunk nearly every moment you've ever spent in my company for years. It was the only way I faced each day."

Brett glanced across the room toward the bar. A glass of wine shimmered in the sunlight. He was nearly certain what was coming but asked anyway. "Why? What was so wrong with your life back then? And why now?"

"I was quite young when we married, and I quickly found out your father was unfaithful to me. He was having an affair when Gary was born. He said now that I was a mother, I was unappealing. He needed to be first in the life of the woman he slept with. Everyone knew about her, though I pretended they didn't. That was how Angelique told me to handle it. She said it was the way men are and the way we cope. But I couldn't cope. So I started drinking."

"She was wrong. Not all men are like him."

She looked at him oddly. "How can you of all people say that? You're just like him. You don't have a faithful bone in your body."

Brett waited for the old pain to lance through him but it didn't. Marcus Costain would have tumbled Deborah Freeman into the nearest bed. Brett Costain hadn't wanted to even touch her.

"No, Mother. I'm not like him. Not at all. I've just been running from life, afraid to love a woman and risk hurting her because everyone told me I was like him. But now I know running isn't an answer. But enough about me. So you began drinking. Then what?"

"I was just pregnant with you. Your father was between women at the time so I suppose I did in a pinch. Gary was starting to toddle and I apparently took him out to the pool. I don't remember, but I passed out. Gary wandered away and a maid found him teetering near the edge of the pool. So they hired Annie and sent me to a clinic until you were born. Then I came home to Bellfield.

"I wasn't allowed to be alone with either of you even though I wasn't drinking anymore. I threatened to divorce Marcus even though it broke my heart, but Angelique said if I did they'd see to it I never saw either of my boys again."

"Where were your parents in all this?"

"Behind Angelique one hundred percent. My drinking and my failure as a wife were a disgrace they didn't want made common knowledge. I should attend to my husband and make myself into his image of the perfect wife.

"So I tried. I attended every function Marcus wanted me to go to and worked constantly at keeping myself in shape. I traveled with him and joined his country club friends for bridge and tennis. He didn't stray as often so I thought I was improving as his wife. But I didn't have time left over for you boys. Then came the Annie incident."

"You once told me you sent her away for her own good. But now it seems you hated her. I take it you saw what he was up to and fired her."

His mother shook her head. "No. And I resented her but I didn't hate her. She took wonderful care of you two. As you said, the two of you were happy. Then she came to me guilt-ridden because she'd let him kiss her and flatter her. I found her another job and sent her away. Your father was furious. So he sent you two off to Aldon."

"My God, Mother, why didn't you fight them then? You'd lost us anyway."

"Annie had been there eight years by then. I'd loved your father to distraction, Brett. And I was suddenly faced with the truth. I'd never been enough for him, and I'd all but abdicated from motherhood to keep him happy. I realized that in trying to be what I thought he wanted, I'd already lost you boys. You didn't cry for me when you left for Aldon. You cried for Annie.''

Brett felt a real tug at his heart for her. But still, he'd only been seven years old. "I'm sorry, Mother, but you weren't my mother. Annie was."

"Which is why I started drinking again that night. I booked my first solo world tour the next day. I found I didn't have to look at my life if I wasn't around here with it staring me in the face."

"So Leigh was right. All these years you've been running from your feelings and wishing things had been different."

His mother looked surprised. "How observant of her. So you understand? All along, at each opportunity I could have taken to fix my life, I took the easy way. That is why I want Annalise. It won't be easy, but she deserves all the advantages being a Costain can give her. And, perhaps this way, I can make up my neglect of Gary through his daughter."

"By destroying her mother?" He glanced at the wineglass. "By endangering Annalise with your drinking?"

She shook her head after following his eyes to the glass on the bar. "I didn't touch it. I haven't had a drink since you called on Gary's birthday. That day, after you hung up, I realized you'd been reaching out to me, and that I had so deadened myself to feelings, I'd just thrown away yet another chance. Some days it's hard, but if I had the baby—''

"Melissa loves her baby," Brett cut in, sitting up straight.

"You'll fight on her side in this, won't you?" his mother whispered.

He nodded. "And I'll never forgive either of you if you don't drop this now. I love them both. I won't let you do this. I can't. Force me to choose and it's my family I'll choose."

"But we're—" She stopped and stared at him. "No. We're not your family anymore, are we?"

"It doesn't have to be that way, and you don't have to quit drinking alone. There are excellent clinics. Call off this suit. I'm sure Melissa won't object to Annalise having a grandmother who's active in her life as long as you don't undermine the value system we're trying to give her."

"She has a grandmother with a most superior value system," his father declared, stalking into the room. "And soon she will live here amidst her heritage where she belongs."

Still a handsome man, with iron-gray hair and character lines that only made him look more distinguished and handsome, Brett could well imagine his father in judge's robes. But not if he didn't back down. Brett would see to it.

"She will be raised to be a proper Costain," his father went on. "Jonathan Tanner assures me we have an excellent case."

Brett stood and stared his father in the eyes. "I'm not letting you do this. Annalise is Melissa's baby. If you force me, I'll try this case in front of more than a judge. I know all about your friends who are putting out feelers for you to run for Judge Alonso's seat on the state Supreme Court. You'll find your lousy parenting skills on the gossip page of every paper in the state. I'll tell them all about Costain family loyalty and how you ridiculed my brother for his happy life. And they'll get to hear every dirty detail about the philanderer who wants to raise Annalise if I have to track down every woman you've cheated with in the last forty years. When I get through with you, the public wouldn't elect you to be a dogcatcher. And when we get to court, I'll testify about my life and my brother's life when we were stuffed into Aldon and left there till we started college.''

"You are a traitor,'' his father thundered.

"And you are an unprincipled womanizing bully whom I hate being related to!''

His mother stood. "And, Marcus, since there will no longer be a woman in the house…'' She smiled at Brett. "And since I have a feeling Melissa will have a husband before you can get them into court, I would guess you don't have a prayer in hell of winning. I'd fold if I were you, darling. And while we're discussing court actions, you should expect to hear from my attorney in the matter of dissolving this farce we've called a marriage all these years. Brett, dear, would you mind lending me your condo in Florida for a while? I think I'd like to go there after I leave the Betty Ford Clinic.''

Brett nodded, proud of his mother for the first time in his life. "Let me know if you need a hand making the arrangements.''

"I think I can do this on my own, son. Thank you for keeping me from making yet another mistake. I'll be in touch.'' He watched her walk to the wet bar and dump the wine in the sink. Then she left, he imagined to start packing.

When she was out of sight, Brett turned back to Marcus Costain and took out his cell phone, pinning the older man with a determined glare. ''Do you call Jonathan Turner or do I call the papers?''

His father accepted the phone without comment.

Chapter Twenty

Melissa walked to the front door again when she saw the flicker of lights along the road through the screen of underbrush and trees. But the car whizzed on by. The first warning chime of the tall French Morbier clock in the foyer sounded. She turned toward it, waiting till a minute later it began striking each hour that had passed. Each beautiful, deep gong resounded through her, shaking the very foundation of her remaining composure.

Twelve.

Midnight.

And still Brett had not called or returned home. Unable to stand the worry for him and the baby a moment longer, she gave in and called him on his cell phone. And instantly got his voice mail. He'd turned it off!

"Call me. I'm frantic," she ordered and hung up,

staring for a long moment at the phone in her hand. She'd kill him!

Once again she went over what she thought his timetable for the day must have been. He'd left the message saying he was headed for Philadelphia at eleven-thirty, but when she'd listened to it again a few hours ago there were road noises in the background. He must have called from his car. That would have put him in the Philadelphia area no later than three o'clock, even if the trip took four hours which was longer than usual. She added to that a generous two hours for meeting with his parents and guessed that he should have been on the road back by five. That should have gotten him home by no later than nine. Nine o'clock had come and gone three hours ago.

Which meant one of several things had happened. Gary's parents hadn't backed down and Brett had needed to meet with their lawyer. Or he'd decided to stay there and return in the morning, not realizing she knew about the custody suit. As awful as their continuing with the lawsuit would be, it was preferable to the only other thing she could think of that would delay him. He'd had an accident.

Across the room, Annalise fussed in her cradle. The poor little thing must sense her mother's worry and there was no doubt in Melissa's mind that the baby missed Brett. There had been confusion in Annalise's eyes when Melissa had settled her on her lap to give her the one bottle a day she got. The bottle Brett always gave her. Then genuine discontent had replaced Annalise's confusion. She usually drained all six ounces of formula, but for Melissa she'd only taken two.

Melissa lifted a fussing Annalise from her cradle,

patting her back. She crooned a tune and promised Brett would be home soon and then everything would be back the way it should be. She paced to the front door again, remembering Izaak's revelation when he'd come to pick up Margaret that afternoon.

Apparently Brett had confided his worry to Izaak that his and Gary's parents would try to take the baby if they believed her standard of living wasn't high enough. His worry had sparked that beautiful barn-raising-like workday in early September.

Izaak had gone on to say that Brett had kept his fear to himself rather than see her live with the same dread that he harbored day after day. She wondered how long he'd worried. All along? Was that why he'd gone to such lengths to get her to accept his help?

She knew how long Brett had known of the immediate threat. Before leaving his house, she'd checked his caller ID record. He'd gotten a call from Bellfield at nearly midnight two nights ago. And Jerry had confirmed what the call had been about with his earlier comment on Brett's mood since that next day. She'd noticed just that morning how tightly wound he was and had asked Brett about it. He'd told her he hadn't been sleeping well. Which meant he was driving that long boring route home exhausted. What if he fell asleep at the wheel? What if he'd already had an accident?

Another hour passed with the gong chiming out the lonely hour of one in the morning. Fifteen minutes later, after the baby had finally fallen asleep, lights flashed in the window as Brett's truck swung around in front of the house. Melissa was on her feet and charging out the door in a heartbeat.

"I'm going to strangle you, Brett Costain!" she called out as she stalked across the yard toward him.

He whirled toward her, clutching the jacket he'd reached back into the cab of the truck to retrieve. "Lissa, please. For God's sake. Let me explain."

He was fine. Fine! He'd had her frantic for hours and he was just fine. Not a scratch on him. Or the damned truck. She'd kill him! Slowly. "Don't you Lissa me!"

"I fixed it. Please. I didn't know what they were up to. Well, I knew they might try it but not for sure. And I wasn't helping them. I wouldn't do that to you. Or Annalise. Please believe me. You and Annalise are my family."

Now she was really ready to take his head off and hand it to him. He thought she had assumed he'd betrayed her? "How could you think that?" she demanded.

Brett stepped back against the truck as if she'd struck him. "I'd started to think of you that way a long time ago," his voice strangled with what sounded like tears. "I'd hoped you'd started to accept me—trust me. At least a little. I—"

"Brett! What are you talking about? Of course, I trust you."

He blinked, clearly not tracking. The poor man was dead on his feet.

"Come inside," she ordered, taking his hand and pulling him across the yard toward the steps. "I think we just got off to a really bad start. You're obviously coming from a different place than I am."

"Hasn't that always been our problem?" he asked bleakly as he trudged up the steps.

''Not anymore it isn't,'' she told him as they entered the foyer.

He blinked. ''Then why do you want to strangle me?''

She pointed to the foyer clock. ''That says one-fifteen. Do you have any idea how worried I've been?''

Brett, looking more confused than ever, reached up to massage the back of his neck. ''I was afraid to call even though I had good news. It's too easy to tell someone to take a hike on the phone. I thought I'd have a better shot at getting you to listen in person. But why didn't you call me? I figured you would if you were willing to talk to me.''

''Because your cell phone is turned off.''

He reached into the pocket of his leather jacket. ''My father must have turned it off when he hung up with Tanner.''

''That's the lawyer he hired?''

''You weren't supposed to know. To worry.''

She pinned him with an annoyed glare. ''Apparently I wasn't supposed to believe in you either.''

Twin flags reddened his cheeks. ''When I found out you knew, I hoped you would. I almost panicked and left to come home then, but I had to stop them. Stop him.''

''How did you find out I knew what was going on?''

''While Mother had me cooling my heels waiting to see her, I remembered my appointment with Jerry. I thought he'd probably just ask you for the key, but then I remembered dropping that damned notice on the living-room table. I called Jerry to make sure you hadn't seen it. He was still there trying to get the heater working right. Since the notice was gone and he said you'd rushed off suddenly, I knew you'd found it. I was afraid of what you'd think. You had good reason not to trust me. After all, I threatened to do exactly the same thing.''

"Do you know how long ago that was, Brett?''

He looked at his watch. "Five months, six days, twelve—''

"Eons," she cut in.

He stared at her, his gaze caressing her face. Then he pulled her against him. "I thought I'd lost you. When you were so angry just now. I thought the worst. I love you so much, Lissa.''

She pulled back and looked up into his eyes. "What took you so long?''

He grinned crookedly. "To realize it or to get home? Just so we're coming from the same place this time,'' he teased.

She hooked her arms around his neck, tears of happiness and relief blurring her vision. "Either. Both. I love you so much I just want to hear your voice. I was so afraid something had happened to you.''

He took her hand and led her to sit on the sofa, secure in his arms. "The trip from hell happened,'' he said on a soul-deep sigh.

What a terrible day he must have had. She put her head on his shoulder and gave him a little hug. "I'm sorry you had to go against your parents. I know you've always wanted a closer relationship with them.''

"I'm not sorry at all, and that wasn't really the hell part,'' he said, then told her all about the incredible revelations of the day, and how he and his mother had stood up to Marcus Costain together. And he told her about his parents' impending divorce and about how he'd promised Pamela he'd ask for a chance for her to be a real grandmother as long as she abided by Melissa's rules.

Then he described the nightmare trip home, the three major accidents at different unavoidable points in the trip, and the fear he'd lived with all night that she thought the worst.

"Something else happened that had nothing to do with Annalise or my parents. While I was waiting to see Mother, Deborah Freeman, the granddaughter of one of my father's clients, stopped into the library to see me. She's probably one of the most beautiful women in the state. In fact, she was elected Miss Pennsylvania several years ago."

Melissa knew who he was talking about. Deborah's divorce had been in the news several months ago. And she was everything Brett had always been attracted to. Melissa sat up, trying to gauge where this was going.

"She was the unattainable goddess of my misspent youth," he said, looking delighted. "And do you know what happened?"

"I can't imagine." But she could. How could any woman not be thoroughly captivated by him?

"She propositioned me. Isn't that great?"

Jealousy stabbed at Melissa. He looked so pleased with himself. But that made no sense in light of his confession of love. She held back from reacting too strongly, but she wasn't about to pretend to be happy that the man she loved had been propositioned by a former beauty queen. "Not really," she said a little sharply.

He grinned. "I didn't think so either. That's what was great. I hated it. I realized I'd never cheat on you because I love you. I couldn't even stand her perfume. And I realized something else. I'm not like my father. Not at all.''

''Well, hallelujah, you finally figured it out.'' Melissa grinned at him.

''You knew. Why didn't you tell me?''

''Watching you these last months, I finally understood a line in the *Wizard of Oz* that always annoyed me. Remember when Dorothy asks Glinda why she hadn't told her that all Dorothy had do to get home was say, 'There's no place like home.' Glinda answered, 'Because you wouldn't have believed me.' Dorothy had to learn for herself that it was true.''

''And I had to learn that I'm not like my father. That I love you so I'd never cheat on you,'' he said, and leaned toward her, cupping her cheek. ''Marry me, Lissa.''

Butterflies instantly invaded her stomach. ''I want to. There's nothing I want more.''

''But?''

''I don't want to live in your world, Brett. I can probably adjust to living farther north again, but I don't want to deal with your family.''

''*You're* my family. *Annalise* is my family. If my mother was being truthful today, maybe she can be part of our family, but that's it. And this is my world now. This is a growing area. I can hang out my shingle across the road. I'll convert one of the bedrooms into an office and use the living room as a waiting room. So start looking for a rolltop desk. I've always wanted one of those.''

Melissa squealed and threw herself into his arms. Brett seemed to understand that as a *yes* and sealed their new life with a kiss.

Epilogue

Brett leaned against the living-room doorjamb and grinned. He'd been doing a lot of that today. His wedding day. Annalise's christening day. And Christmas Eve. They'd decided to roll all three celebrations into one.

Both Melissa and the baby wore creamy-looking velvet dresses trimmed in antique lace. In the corner was a Christmas tree Lindsey Tanner and Melissa had decorated. It looked more like a wedding cake than the cake did. It was lit with white lights that looked like candles. The ornaments were pearly white and silver bells. Cream-colored ribbons trailed down the branches from a ring of bows just below the skirt of a silvery angel with golden hair. Potted red and white poinsettias throughout the house finished off the holiday theme.

Because his closest friend other than Melissa was

Lindsey Tanner, and Melissa's closest friend other
than him was Hunter Long, they'd asked them to be
their witnesses and godparents to Annalise. It might
not have been a traditional ceremony, their vows said
before a glowing fire—the maid of honor standing
next to the groom and the best man next to the bride.
The bride hadn't carried a bouquet but a baby in a
matching dress who was christened over an antique
washstand after they'd exchanged vows.

An unorthodox ceremony to be sure, but it would
be a very traditional wedding night. And he was having a hard time not asking the few guests remaining
to get the hell home. He wanted his wife in the worst
way.

The night of her six-week postnatal checkup she'd
sweetly invited him to stay the night. And he'd turned
her down. Flat. She'd waited twenty-eight years for
him and their wedding, he'd told her, he could wait
three weeks. She'd kissed him and thanked him for
understanding her so well and he'd fallen in love all
over again. He'd suffered for that noble gesture every
second since, just thinking about the bliss to come—
the bliss he'd turned down. But still, he wasn't sorry.
There was something to be said for anticipation.

But mercy, why didn't they leave?

It wasn't as if there were many guests left. The
Amish families had left hours ago, having stayed only
a short time. He'd just returned from seeing several
of Melissa's high-school friends to their cars, so only
his mother, Lindsey and Hunter and Bobby and Shelly
Sue Cook were left. He watched Melissa hand the
baby to his mother and nearly groaned. Was there no
end in sight?

"You look like a man about to crawl out of his

skin,'' Hunter Long said, grinning as he came back in from the kitchen. He held out a glass of wine.

Brett accepted it, but didn't smile in return. "Go home," he grumbled, drawing a bark of laughter from the sheriff.

Hunter's laughter drew Melissa's attention. She handed a baby bottle to his mother and walked toward them. Brett abandoned his relaxed pose, straightening away from the door frame.

She smiled up at him and pointed upward at the mistletoe hanging above his head. Brett handed the wine back to Hunter without taking his eyes off Melissa, then he took his wife in his arms.

The foyer clock gave off its warning bong and her smile widened. "Merry Christmas, Mr. Costain," she whispered as his lips neared hers.

Her scent wrapped around him and the feel of her soft body nestled close to his set his senses ablaze. Her lips under his opened and he deepened the kiss. She tasted of wedding cake, champagne and a fire that was all Melissa. She was everything he'd ever wanted or needed in a woman and she was all his.

At least she would be soon.

Brett broke the kiss as the final stroke of midnight echoed through the house. "If they don't go soon, I'm going to toss them all out. I want you," he whispered.

"That would be awfully impolite," she told him and kept her arms looped around his neck. "I'm about to put the baby down for the night. They'll go soon enough after that."

"And then you're mine, Mrs. Costain." Brett left his hands linked at the small of her back and decided then and there that he wasn't letting go of her again unless one of them had to take care of the baby.

"And then I'm all yours, Mr. Costain," she promised. Her smile evolved from a warm glow of promised heat to an alluring blaze that threatened to burn him to a cinder right where he stood.

Just then Lindsey said, "Well, Merry Christmas, everyone."

He and Melissa looked over and they were all standing in front of the tree with wineglasses in their hands, except his mother who was on the settee in front of them, feeding Annalise.

"I'd like to propose a toast," Lindsey continued. "To new beginnings, bright futures and love. May we all have all three."

The two other couples tapped glasses, but he and Melissa sealed the wish with a kiss.

"And now—" Hunter said "—before our groom tosses us out on our collective rears, I think it's time to hit the road. I'll drop Lindsey and your mother off across the road."

"Yeah, my mom's with the baby so we'd better get on home anyway," Shelly Sue Cook said as she put down her wineglass and reached out her hand for Bobby. "This was a real special wedding."

Goodbyes took too long as far as Brett was concerned, but he tried not to show it. Then Melissa took the baby up to tuck her in bed and Brett rushed around, setting the scene he'd been imagining for hours.

Just as he finished, Melissa descended the staircase. "She's all tucked in. I think all the excitement wore her out."

Brett met her at the bottom step and took her hand, placing a kiss in her palm. "Good. I have plans that don't include her for a few hours at least,'' he told his bride.

''Plans?'' she teased. ''Why, whatever could they be?''

''They involve that new quilt Margaret and the other ladies made for our wedding gift.''

''The wedding-ring quilt?''

Brett nodded and led her toward the living room. ''And the magical glow of the tree,'' he continued, flipping off the foyer light, leaving the house in darkness except for the soft glow of the tree and the crackling fire. ''Soft Christmas music in the background and a little love nest just for us,'' he finished as he led her across the room.

Melissa smiled. He'd thought of everything, she thought as his lips took hers. His tongue came out to trace the seam of her lips and she was shocked to hear a strangled moan come from the back of her throat. Could there be too much anticipation? Too much pent-up need and desire?

''Lissa,'' he whispered; his breath on her ear felt hotter than the heat of the fire at that moment. She wove her fingers into his hair and held on to sanity by a thin thread when she felt her zipper whisper down her spine. She gasped, breaking the kiss and shivered as his fingers moved downward to the small of her back, caressing her naked skin.

''You will never know how relieved I was to find out that there was a zipper hiding under all those buttons. What are they there for? To torture the poor groom all day?''

She chuckled. ''I think so. Did it work?''

''Unnecessary,'' he breathed against her ear.

He wasn't telling her anything. Had his voice, which had gone all rough and husky, not given him away, she'd still have felt his thick arousal through the layers of silk, crinoline and velvet between them. Those layers and his own were suddenly more than she could stand. She stepped back and grinned up at him. Besides, he wasn't the only one who could set a scene.

"What's that sexy smile all abou— Oh, Lissa," he croaked, his eyes suddenly black as night as she dropped the dress from her shoulders. With it fell everything but her bra, panties and lace-topped hose.

She stepped out of the huge pile of clothing and picked it up, flinging it into a chair, then kicked out of her shoes before reaching for the buttons of his shirt. "I can't tell you how glad I am that we decided you should wear a suit. No studs," she said as she undid one small pearly button then moved slowly on to the next and then the next. Brett's breathing grew less steady as she progressed.

He ended that game by popping the last few buttons and pulling her into his arms. His lips took hers in a kiss that spread fire to her very core. There was no part of her that didn't crave his touch, and within minutes there was no part of her he hadn't touched.

The setting was no less perfect than the last time he'd hovered over her, kissing her, caressing her, laving her breasts with his ravenous tongue but this time—this time there was more than desire and hunger and need. This time the dark words he used to urge her higher were interspersed with, "I love you. I've waited a lifetime for you. I don't think I could live without you—without this."

And this time nothing she said or asked or did

stopped him from making them one. From changing them from one man and one woman into husband and wife. This time there was no rush to retreat and return to an old life. There was only sweet aftermath and loving the night away.

* * * * *

*Look for Kate Welsh's next
heartwarming and
inspirational love story:*

HOME TO SAFE HARBOR

*(on sale June 2003)
It's the exciting conclusion
to the Love Inspired*
SAFE HARBOR *miniseries.*

Turn the page for a sneak preview...

Chapter One

Reverend Justine Clemens stood frozen before the entire congregation of First Peninsula Church, managing to hold a smile in place through sheer determination. In her hands, she held the plaque she'd just accepted amid thunderous applause. Clearly, everyone thought she should be thrilled.

They were certainly thrilled.

She was devastated.

The sign on her new office door would not read Reverend Justine Clemens—Assistant Pastor. That's what she'd thought Reverend Burns and the board had meant when they'd asked her to stay on permanently to assist him. Instead the plaque she now held tightly clutched in her hands read Reverend Justine Clemens—Women and Youth Pastor.

Once again she'd been relegated to a traditional role for women in the church. Once again she was on the road to having no one and nothing to call her own.

When Reverend Burns retired—and at seventy how far off could that be?—she'd thought these people would be her flock. That they would look to her for guidance. Be her family.

The corners of the brass plaque bit into her hands and she managed to relax her trembling grip just a little. But, as she did, she also had to blink back the tears that threatened to give her away. Reverend Burns had just handed her what he clearly thought of as first prize but she knew it to be the honorable mention it was.

He stood next to her at the reception following the service, smiling and looking more like a man of sixty these days.

"You're upset," Reverend Burns said when there was a break in the line of parishioners who'd come over to congratulate her on her new role. His brows were drawn together in a worried frown.

Justine started and felt a blush heat her face. If he knew, did everyone else?

"Relax. I doubt anyone else noticed but I know you too well to be fooled by that pasted-on smile. What is it, dear?"

Justine had never been able to hide the truth from Reverend Burns, not from that first day he'd caught her cutting school and enjoying a cigarette behind the gazebo in Safe Harbor Park with her new friends.

"I thought you asked me to stay on to be your assistant."

"That's exactly what you will be."

Justine turned the plaque she still held toward him. "But it's a ministry limited to women and children."

The older man sighed, shaking his head slightly. "You're still seeing the glass half-empty, Justine. You are an absolute wonder with the teens and younger women, not to mention the little ones. You relate to them in a way I find I no longer can. They make up a good portion of the congregation. I want them going to you for help. You can do a lot of good.''

She felt her face heat, embarrassed by what sounded like selfish motives. The words tumbled out. "I thought I was being put in position to take your place one day. And I know you and the board wouldn't have limited the scope of my ministry if you had confidence in me that I could replace you."

"But we do have confidence in you," Reverend Burns said gently. "You must seek God's plan for your life, dear, not your own. I very much fear that is what you've been doing all along." He held up his hand to stop her automatic defense. "I'm not saying your call to the ministry wasn't real. I'm saying that maybe He has something for you that you're blind to. I don't know what His plan is, but for now why not do the job He's sent you and see what comes of it?"

Justine nodded jerkily, trying to hold back the emotions that surged in her. She could see the wisdom in his words, but following his advice would be a struggle.

"Excuse me, Reverend Clemens. Reverend Burns," a deep voice interrupted her struggle for composure. "I wonder if I might have a word with you before the kids descend on us."

Past hurts and new ones flew out of Justine's mind when she followed the sound of that husky voice to a point just over her head.

It was *him*.

At five foot ten she wasn't used to looking up at many people. At least not as far as she had to look up right now. She found herself snared by eyes even a deeper brown than her own. They were nearly obsidian. A rich dark chocolate.

For weeks she'd seen Matthew Trent around town and in church and now she had a voice to put with that hauntingly handsome face. A dangerous combination of tall, dark and gorgeous, he was the new chief of police and he distracted Justine every time she noticed him. Once, even in the middle of a sermon!

No man had ever affected her the way he did. No man had ever taken her eyes off her ministry or made her heart pump harder with the sound of his voice. There were times she wished she had the courage to take a chance on love and a family but those things were not for her. She couldn't be a pastor *and* a mother. Leading a church was too demanding. It wouldn't be fair to the children. And besides that, she couldn't be a mother without first being a wife and she'd never trust any man with her heart. She'd watched first-hand what could happen to a woman who loved and lost. Especially when the man appeared to be all that was brave, heroic and trustworthy.

*   *   *   *   *

V™ Silhouette®

SPECIAL EDITION™

presents the final title in

VICTORIA PADE'S
heartwarming miniseries

Baby Times 3

Three bachelor brothers surrender to the power of love...and revel in the bond between father and baby.

Available now...

THE BABY SURPRISE
SE #1544, June 2003

A confirmed bachelor gets the shock of his lifetime when he learns he might be a daddy!

And if you missed the first two titles, look for

HER BABY SECRET, SE #1503, 11/02
MAYBE MY BABY, SE #1515, 01/03

Available at your favorite retail outlet.

V™ Silhouette®

Where love comes alive™

Visit Silhouette at www.eHarlequin.com   SSEBTTMINI

In June 2003

Silhouette Books invites you to share a blessed event

Baby Love

Baby
JOAN ELLIOTT PICKART

VICTORIA PADE

Love

A Child Will Change Everything

She had promised to raise her sister's baby as her own, with no interference from the baby's insufferable father. But that was before she met that darkly handsome, if impossible, man! He was someone she was having a hard time ignoring. Don't miss Joan Elliott Pickart's *Mother at Heart*.

Their passionate marriage was over, their precious dreams in ashes. And then a swelling in her belly made one couple realize that one of their dreams would yet see the light of day. Look for Victoria Pade's *Baby My Baby*.

Available at your favorite retail outlet.

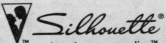

Silhouette®

Where love comes alive™

Visit Silhouette at www.eHarlequin.com

BR2BL

**Silhouette Desire
presents the continuation of**

LONE STAR
LSCC
COUNTRY CLUB
EST. 1923

Where Texas society reigns supreme—
and appearances are *everything!*

Shameless

(SD #1513)

by

ANN MAJOR

On sale June 2003

A lonely ex-marine
must decide:
Can he snub the
heartbreaking siren
he's sworn to
forget...or
will he give
in to her mind-
blowing seduction...
and a last chance
at love?

*Available at your
favorite retail outlet.*

Silhouette®
Where love comes alive™

Visit Silhouette at www.eHarlequin.com

SDLSCCS

eHARLEQUIN.com

Calling all aspiring writers!
Learn to craft the perfect romance novel
with our useful tips and tools:

- Take advantage of our **Romance Novel Critique Service** for detailed advice from romance professionals.

- Use our **message boards** to connect with writers, published authors and editors.

- Enter our **Writing Round Robin—** you could be published online!

- Learn many writing hints in our **Top 10 Writing lists!**

- **Guidelines** for Harlequin or Silhouette novels—what our editors *really* look for.

Learn more about romance writing from the experts—

visit www.eHarlequin.com today!

INTLTW

If you enjoyed what you just read,
then we've got an offer you can't resist!

Take 2 bestselling
love stories FREE!

Plus get a FREE surprise gift!

Clip this page and mail it to Silhouette Reader Service™

IN U.S.A.
3010 Walden Ave.
P.O. Box 1867
Buffalo, N.Y. 14240-1867

IN CANADA
P.O. Box 609
Fort Erie, Ontario
L2A 5X3

YES! Please send me 2 free Silhouette Special Edition® novels and my free surprise gift. After receiving them, if I don't wish to receive anymore, I can return the shipping statement marked cancel. If I don't cancel, I will receive 6 brand-new novels every month, before they're available in stores! In the U.S.A., bill me at the bargain price of $3.99 plus 25¢ shipping and handling per book and applicable sales tax, if any*. In Canada, bill me at the bargain price of $4.74 plus 25¢ shipping and handling per book and applicable taxes**. That's the complete price and a savings of at least 10% off the cover prices—what a great deal! I understand that accepting the 2 free books and gift places me under no obligation ever to buy any books. I can always return a shipment and cancel at any time. Even if I never buy another book from Silhouette, the 2 free books and gift are mine to keep forever.

235 SDN DNUR
335 SDN DNUS

Name	(PLEASE PRINT)	
Address	Apt.#	
City	State/Prov.	Zip/Postal Code

* Terms and prices subject to change without notice. Sales tax applicable in N.Y.
** Canadian residents will be charged applicable provincial taxes and GST.
   All orders subject to approval. Offer limited to one per household and not valid to
   current Silhouette Special Edition® subscribers.
   ® are registered trademarks of Harlequin Books S.A., used under license.

SPED02   ©1998 Harlequin Enterprises Limited

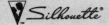

SPECIAL EDITION™

and

bestselling author
LAURIE PAIGE

introduce a new series about seven cousins—
bound by blood, honor and tradition—who bring
a whole new meaning to "family reunion"!

SEVEN DEVILS

This time, the Daltons are the good guys....

"Laurie Paige doesn't miss..."
—*New York Times* bestselling author
Catherine Coulter

"It is always a joy to savor the consistent
excellence of this outstanding author."
—*Romantic Times*

Available at your favorite retail outlet.

Where love comes alive™

Coming in June 2003 from

▼ Silhouette®

INTIMATE MOMENTS™

The action continues with the men—
and women—of the Omega Agency
in Merline Lovelace's

CODE NAME: DANGER

To Love a Thief (IM #1225)

Omega director Nick Jensen has a secret
past—one that's threatening to catch up
with him in a big way. His partner in
"crime"—beautiful agent Mackenzie Blair.

Code Name: Danger:
Because love is a risky business...

Available at your favorite retail outlet.

▼ Silhouette®
Where love comes alive™

Visit Silhouette at www.eHarlequin.com

SIMTLAT

√ Silhouette®

COMING NEXT MONTH

#1543 ONE IN A MILLION—Susan Mallery
Hometown Heartbreakers

FBI negotiator Nash Harmon was in town looking for long-lost family, not romance. But meeting Stephanie Wynne, the owner of the B & B where he was staying and a single mother of three, changed his plans. Neither could deny their desires, but would responsibilities to career and family keep them apart?

#1544 THE BABY SURPRISE—Victoria Pade
Baby Times Three

Wildlife photographer Devon Tarlington got the surprise of his life when Keely Gilhooley showed up on his doorstep with a baby. *His* baby. Or so she claimed. Keely was merely doing her job by locating the father of this abandoned infant. She hadn't expected Devon, or the simmering attraction between them....

#1545 THE ONE AND ONLY—Laurie Paige
Seven Devils

There was something mysterious about new to Lost Valley nurse-assistant Shelby Wheeling.... Dynamic doctor Beau Dalton was intrigued as much by her secrets as he was by the woman. Would their mutual desire encourage Shelby to open up, or keep Beau at arm's length?

#1546 HEARD IT THROUGH THE GRAPEVINE—Teresa Hill

A preacher's daughter was not supposed to be pregnant and alone. But that's exactly what Cathie Baldwin was...until Matthew Monroe, the onetime local bad boy, came along and offered the protection of his name and wealth. But who would protect *him* from falling in love...with Cathie *and* the baby?

#1547 ALASKAN NIGHTS—Judith Lyons

Being trapped in the Alaskan wilds with her charter client was not pilot Winnie Taylor's idea of a good time, no matter how handsome he was. Nor was it Rand Michaels's. For he had to remind himself that as a secret mercenary for Freedom Rings he was here to obtain information...not to fall in love.

#1548 A MOTHER'S SECRET—Pat Warren

Her nephew was in danger. And Sara Morgan had nowhere else to turn but to police detective Graham Kincaid. Now, following a trail left by the kidnapper, would Sara and Graham's journey lead them to the boy...and to each other?

SSECNM0503